The Escort

NIGHTS SERIES BOOK TWO

A.M. SALINGER

COPYRIGHT

The Escort (Nights Series Book 2)
Copyright © 2017 by A.M. Salinger
All rights reserved.
Registered with the US Copyright Office.
Second paperback edition: 2024
ISBN: 978-1-9996184-1-4

www.AMSalinger.com
shop.adstarrling.com

Edited by www.ElfwerksEditing.com
Cover Design by A.M. Salinger

BOOKS BY A.M. SALINGER

Nights

One Night - 1

The Escort - 2

Tokyo Heat - 3

Sweet Obsession - 4

Sweet Possession - 5

The Proposition - 6

Undisclosed - 7

Hush - 8

One Day - 9

Nights Series Short Story Collection

Twilight Falls

Alex - 1

Carter - 2

Hunter - 3

Wyatt - 4

Drake - 5

Tristan - 6

Miles - 7

Urban Fantasy Romance written as

Ava Marie Salinger

Fallen Messengers

Fractured Souls - 1

Spellbound - 2

Edge Lines - 3

Oathbreaker - 4

Harbinger - 5

Crimson Skies - 6

Wicked - Fallen Messengers Short Story Collection

CHAPTER ONE

Joe Cavendish swallowed a groan as he stared at the tantalizing ass ten feet from him.

That little tease. I'm sure he's doing it on purpose.

"Do you have to be on your hands and knees for that?" he said with a sigh. "It's not exactly as if I'm a fucking slave driver, you know. I did just buy one of those ridiculously expensive mopping robots for the staff to use."

Ethan Skye looked over his shoulder and narrowed his eyes at Joe where the latter sat at the bar drinking a coffee.

"Your robot knows dick about oak floors. And I'm not cleaning. I'm fixing the scratch that asshole made when he dragged that metal case in here yesterday. I mean, who the fuck lugs that kind of shit around? And, FYI, his gin tasted like crap, so we're not getting it."

Joe arched an eyebrow and glanced around *Saron's* opulent interior.

"You do realize I own the place, right?"

Ethan gave the floor a final wipe with a polishing cloth and rose to his feet.

"And I'm your best bartender. What's your point?"

He placed his toolbox on the counter and studied Joe with a haughty expression.

Joe couldn't deny the truth of his words. Although *Saron* had rapidly gained a reputation as the most exclusive gay club in Tokyo since he first opened for business four years ago, part of its phenomenal success of late had a lot to do with the stunning blond with the captivating green eyes who had waltzed into his club eleven months ago and demanded he give him a job.

It wasn't every day that someone made Joe Cavendish look at them twice. Ethan Skye had made him look twice, three times, and a dozen more after that.

That fact alone should have had Joe running hell-for-leather in the other direction. He couldn't recall the last time his body had had such an immediate, visceral reaction to a stranger, even during his years working as an escort. Still, he'd found himself unable to deny the demand in the mesmerizing green eyes that had bored so intensely into him and had reluctantly invited the young man back for an interview the week after.

Surprise had darted through Joe when Ethan had pulled out his résumé and asked if he could do the interview there and then, offering the club owner a foretaste of his bossy nature. Joe had taken the professional, double-sided sheet and studied it with a frown.

"Says here you're a Stanford business graduate."

He'd looked up into Ethan's cool expression. "Why the hell would you want to be a bartender in Shinjuku?"

"I'm not made for a city job. Besides, I almost flunked business school."

Joe had bought that cock-and-bull story about as much as he believed in Santa Claus. He'd been around the block enough times to tell when somebody was harboring secrets. After all, he had some pretty dark ones of his own.

Ethan had passed his interview with flying colors and didn't even blink when Joe challenged him to make *Saron*'s trademark cocktail and give it his own personal twist. One sip of the intoxicating drink Ethan made was all it took for Joe to realize he shouldn't let the cocky blond slip out of his hands and into a competitor's clutches.

In the months since Ethan had been at *Saron*, the bartender had become a key member of his staff. He got on with everyone, including the normally taciturn doormen, and had charmed all the patrons with his quick wit and exquisite drinks. The fact that he was goddamn easy on the eye didn't hurt either.

Had Joe known at the time the fresh hell he would be inviting into his life by giving Ethan the bartending job, he would probably have refused the young man. Joe knew a lot of the club's patrons would kill to get their hands on *Saron*'s newest bartender. Not only was Ethan drop-dead gorgeous, he had also been blessed with a naturally athletic physique; just enough muscle not to be brawny and the entire package perfectly toned in all the right places.

Places Joe had been aching to touch for months.

As days turned to weeks and weeks to months, the spark that had been there between them from the start had ignited into a maelstrom of full-blown lust that had Joe's cock aching most times he came within twenty feet of the alluring bartender.

It didn't help that he'd once walked in on Ethan in the staff changing room and gotten an eyeful of the delicious body he'd been fantasizing about. Joe had wondered for days afterward how many men had kissed the mole he'd glimpsed on Ethan's right hip, just above his low-riding briefs. And how many more had tasted his honey skin and claimed his tight ass.

The fact that Ethan wouldn't refuse Joe made their situation all the more bittersweet. He had made it abundantly clear he was gay from the first day he started working at *Saron*. And just as Joe's eyes seemed to gravitate to Ethan whenever they were in the same room, Ethan always tracked him with his heated gaze in return.

But even though Ethan had turned the carefully ordered life Joe had built over the last few years upside down and had become the source of some of Joe's filthiest fantasies, hooking up with the young man was the one thing the club owner wouldn't let happen. He'd had his fingers burned once before when he'd mixed business with pleasure, and he'd made it a rule never to do so again.

Unfortunately, Ethan didn't seem to agree with him on the clear dividing lines Joe had set from the start of their working relationship. He was constantly pushing at the boundaries, testing the limits of Joe's patience and his raging libido.

Just as he was doing right now.

"I've spoken to our regular gin supplier," Joe said with a grunt. "It seems the shortfall we're experiencing is going to last some time. We need to find another company to get our stock from." He hesitated. "Eveline can probably—"

"No!" Ethan snapped. The mere mention of the name Joe had just uttered made the bartender grit his teeth. "Give me a day. I'll get you another supplier by tomorrow."

Joe bit back a frustrated sigh at Ethan's stormy expression. He still didn't know how Ethan had discovered his connection with *Le Secret*, the internationally renowned, upscale escort service Joe used to work for before he started *Saron*. It sure as hell hadn't come from one of Joe's other staff, who knew nothing of his past.

The brainchild of Eveline Claude, a former escort and professional dominatrix, *Le Secret* catered only to the wealthiest of clientele—from politicians and royalty, to movie stars and billionaires. With clubs in five cities around the world, the business advertised itself as offering a strictly social service, even though a lot of its clients were really after sex. Eveline had always made it clear that what happened behind closed doors was a private matter between client and escort, and she'd kicked out plenty of both over the years who hadn't followed the strict rules she laid out for her clubs.

Though he was no longer in Eveline's employ, Joe still accepted the odd gig from her. After all, she was the one who had saved him from the nightmare he'd been living in when he worked in the shady underworld of New York's sex and strip clubs between the ages of fifteen and twenty-four. He also owed her big time for the loan she'd given him to set up his own business, money he'd paid back within a year of opening *Saron*'s doors.

That most people would find his background and previous lifestyle distasteful was not something that kept Joe awake at night. Yet Ethan's reaction when he'd first challenged Joe about the jobs he still took on for *Le Secret*'s owner had stung. It wasn't judgment Joe had read in Ethan's eyes that day. It was resentment and frustration that Joe could willingly sleep with a complete stranger but not lay a finger on him.

Joe considered the young man presently scowling at him; he knew not to disbelieve the words he had just spoken. Ethan had made similar promises in the past on the rare occasions Joe had been in a fix and always delivered on them. Joe narrowed his eyes.

"I'd really like to know who your source is."

The corner of Ethan's mouth lifted in an insolent smile that made Joe want to kiss him hard.

"I'm afraid I would have to kill you if I revealed that information."

A bark of laughter left Joe's lips at the threat. His groin tightened at the torrid image that flashed across his inner vision. Of Ethan slowly and sweetly killing him with his exquisite body while he straddled Joe and rode his cock, his sexy hips undulating with every hard thrust of Joe's dick while his filthy mouth opened on throaty cries and moans.

"Here, pour me another coffee."

Ethan rolled his eyes. "Yes, master."

Joe swallowed another groan.

Yup, he's doing it deliberately.

CHAPTER TWO

ETHAN FROZE WHEN HE CAME OUT THE BACK DOOR AND saw the red rose resting on the lid of the trash can.

He stared at it before scanning the alley behind *Saron,* his gaze probing the shadows, searching for a watchful figure. Like the dozen times before, he saw no one. He hesitated before carefully picking up the stem.

The flower was wrapped in cellophane and had a note attached. Ethan didn't have to read it to know its contents. It would be the same anonymous message of admiration and thinly veiled lust he'd received since the beginning. When he found the first note on the club's mahogany counter at the end of a shift four months ago, Ethan had put it down as a prank by one of the staff. A week later, he discovered another note carefully tucked behind the bar.

His unease had slowly grown as more notes materialized. Though he'd subtly questioned the doormen and other bartenders, no one had ever seen the person who'd left him the messages. It wasn't until the day a letter appeared in his mailbox back at his apartment building that Ethan had finally grasped the chilling truth: he'd gained himself a stalker.

He'd considered contacting the cops and even discussed the matter with his accountant and the latter's brother, a detective in the Tokyo Metropolitan Police Department. Though the man had been sympathetic to Ethan's plight, he'd made it clear that they couldn't take any action unless there was a clear threat to Ethan's life.

Ethan had wondered briefly then whether he should bring Joe into the loop. But the thought of having to rely on the man he so clearly wanted but who continued to reject him left too much of a bitter aftertaste in Ethan's mouth for him to seek his help. Besides, Ethan had his pride. He wouldn't lower himself in front of the bastard he'd fallen in love with at first sight almost a year ago and who had frustrated the hell out of him every single day since. And what Joe would make of his lies, if he ever uncovered them, was not something Ethan took lightly.

Truth was, he'd misled Joe when he'd walked into *Saron* and demanded that bartending job. Ethan hadn't flunked business school. He'd fucking aced it, graduating summa cum laude and top of his class at Stanford. At the age of twenty-eight, his stocks and shares portfolio pretty much guaranteed him a lifetime of luxury.

But rather than live the decadent existence of a

millionaire, Ethan chose to donate most of his money to a bunch of charities and other philanthropic enterprises, his biggest contribution going to a nonprofit organization that supported street kids around the world.

It wasn't his family's wealth that had landed Ethan a place at Stanford. It was the scholarship he'd worked his ass off to get while still doing evening shifts as a busboy in the dive bar where his aunt used to waitress that had given him a chance at a better life.

Ethan had never known his parents. His mother had died from late childbirth complications when he was barely a week old, and from what his aunt had deduced, he was the result of a one-night stand. His aunt had never been able to drag out the identity of Ethan's father from her own sister before she passed away.

Though they had been dirt poor, life with his only living relative had been loving and fulfilling. Ethan couldn't have asked for a better upbringing and it was thanks to his aunt that he had grown to be the successful, levelheaded man he now was. She'd even realized he was gay before he became aware of it himself and had helped him embrace his homosexuality to the fullest. Although Ethan had had to put his foot down when she started slipping gay sex guides under his pillow.

Shortly after Ethan made his first million, he'd forced his aunt to take early retirement and bought her a mansion in Baja California. They still saw each other every Thanksgiving, even after Ethan's move to Tokyo, and he couldn't have been more thrilled when she finally settled down with the retired college professor who lived down the road from her.

Ethan had been considering returning to the States to be closer to her when life had thrown him a curveball, also known as Joe.

To this day, Joe still thought their first meeting was the time Ethan walked into *Saron* and asked for a bartending job. He didn't know Ethan had come there a couple of months before with his accountant and had fallen head over heels for the brooding club owner the moment he saw him walk into the bar.

Heads had turned and the noise level had fallen when Joe strolled down the steps and headed casually across the club. The sexual thrill that had coursed through Ethan as he stared at the tall, hard-bodied, dark-haired man with the hooded hazel eyes and sexy stubble had had his dick throbbing for the rest of that night. Ethan had had plenty of bed partners over the years. But never before had he had the gut-wrenching, animal reaction he had experienced with Joe with any of them.

He'd been back to *Saron* several times after that and realized that what he was feeling for Joe was more than just lust. And so, like every goal he'd ever set himself to accomplish in his life, Ethan had gone after what he wanted with his usual energy and zeal, crafting a careful plan to infiltrate *Saron* and capture the club owner's heart.

From what his accountant had told him, Joe was the type to fuck them and leave them. Although Ethan wanted nothing more than to be in Joe's arms and under that rock-hard body, there was no way he intended to become another notch in that magnificent man's bedpost.

His accountant had choked on his iced latte when Ethan first told him his intentions. Though he'd warned him against it, Ethan had still gone ahead with his plan to pursue Joe. It'd helped that he'd bartended to pay his living expenses while he was attending Stanford and even won an award for his skills.

Eleven months after his first shift at *Saron* and Ethan was nowhere closer to getting in the man's pants. The fact that Joe stringently adhered to his no-mixing-business-with-pleasure rule and refused to lay a finger on any of his patrons or staff had not discouraged Ethan. Sure, it meant he spent most of his hours at the club horny as hell and had jerked off to the mental image of Joe so many times the guy's name ought to be tattooed to his dick, but it had not dissuaded him from his program of action, which was to tempt the hell out of Joe until he snapped.

The fruit, when it finally fell, would be all the sweeter—that, Ethan was certain of.

The only thing that had the potential to throw a wrench in the works was the discovery he'd made a few months back. That Joe still did the odd job for Madame Claude, the owner of the notorious *Le Secret* chain of upscale escort clubs. The fact that Joe clearly wasn't doing it for the money was what had infuriated Ethan the most. It indicated that the woman had some sort of hold on Joe that Ethan didn't know about.

And, now there's the stalker too. When it rains, it fucking pours.

A chill ran down Ethan's spine as he studied the flower and the note. He crushed them both and shoved them in the trash can.

CHAPTER THREE

JOE STRETCHED HIS ARMS ABOVE HIS HEAD AND YAWNED. It was five in the afternoon and almost time to open up shop.

He'd been up since ten and had spent most of the day doing his accounts. The final figures had sent a warm feeling of satisfaction coursing through him; he was pleased to see the healthy profit the club had made over the last month. He looked out the window and watched the dying rays of the sun streak across the patches of sky visible between the Shinjuku high rises.

Though he could easily afford to rent a place where his best friend, Cam Sorvino, lived in the exclusive Ebisu area of Tokyo, Joe wouldn't have traded his tiny apartment above *Saron* for anything in the world. It was the first place he'd ever owned outright and the only true home he'd ever known.

He rose from his desk and grabbed his jacket; he'd made it a habit to go for a walk at this time every day since he first got the keys to *Saron*. He headed out the door and took the stairs that led to the back of the club.

SHIT.

Ethan picked up speed, his gaze on the alley exit some hundred feet ahead.

He'd taken this shortcut to *Saron* plenty of times before and never had any trouble. Ethan cursed himself when he realized he'd ended up in this situation through his own fault.

He'd found another note in his mailbox when he returned to his apartment in the early hours of that morning. Though Ethan suspected it had come with the second delivery of the day, he'd still checked his place for signs of breaking and entering and slept fitfully until after midday. He had all but forgotten about the note until five minutes ago, when he was making his way back to the club for his evening shift.

The sensation of being followed had started as a faint itch on the back of his neck. By the time he'd entered the series of back alleys that cut across Shinjuku to the club, Ethan was convinced someone was tailing him.

That asshole was probably waiting for me somewhere outside my building.

He'd stopped and looked over his shoulder time and time again but had seen no one in the shadows rapidly growing around him. Still, he couldn't shake the icy feeling skittering across his skin.

The sound of a foot kicking against a can reached Ethan's ears a second later. He froze in his tracks before slowly twisting on his heels. He stared into the gloom, his pulse racing.

A figure stood watching him from behind a dumpster some sixty feet away.

Oh, fuck.

Ethan turned and ran, fear roiling his stomach and sending a wave of bile up his throat. The alley exit blurred ahead of him as panic constricted his vision and his rib cage. He gritted his teeth and pounded the asphalt, refusing to give in to the terror threatening to drown him.

A choked cry bubbled past his lips when he finally escaped the suffocating confines of the passage and came out onto a main road. His breath locked in his lungs in the next moment as he slammed into someone.

꠲

JOE GRUNTED WHEN A MAN DARTED OUT OF AN ALLEYWAY and plowed into him, bowling them both to the ground. He landed on his back with a curse, the other guy on top of him.

"Hey, asshole, watch where you're—"

The rest of Joe's rebuke died in his throat when he registered the identity of the man lying against him.

Ethan's expression was wild-eyed and ashen, his pupils dark and dilated in a sea of green, his breaths coming hard and fast. Alarm filled Joe when he felt the tremors running through Ethan's body.

He sat up and gripped Ethan's shoulders.

"Hey, are you okay?"

Ethan startled. Recognition dawned on his face. He jerked back from Joe's touch and landed hard on his ass. Joe's heart twisted painfully at the physical rejection. He had barely begun to register his own shocking reaction when he saw dread wash across Ethan's features. Ethan twisted and stared over his shoulder toward the mouth of the alley.

Joe's stomach plummeted, unease slowly filling him.

"Ethan?"

Ethan blinked and turned to look at Joe. His gaze dropped to his trembling hands where they lay in his lap. He sat with his legs out and his head bowed, unheeding of the passersby staring at them.

"Shit," he murmured hoarsely.

Deep beneath the fear Joe could read in Ethan's voice, he detected a thread of anger. Joe frowned, trepidation sending his pulse racing.

"What the hell is going on?"

❧

"*You fucking idiot!*"

Ethan winced and wrapped his hands around the steaming cup of coffee. He and Joe were in the staff room back at the club. Though the hot drink warmed Ethan's skin, it had yet to take away the coldness still coursing through him. He sat on the couch with his shoulders hunched and quietly bore the wrath of the angry man pacing the floor in front of him.

"Why the hell didn't you say anything?" Joe growled. "*Damn it*, Ethan, you could have been hurt!"

Ethan swallowed a sigh. He deserved that one too.

Joe suddenly stilled, his hand stopping midway through raking his hair.

"Do any of the staff know about this?"

Ethan glanced at Joe's stormy expression and shook his head, grateful he hadn't involved his coworkers.

"I asked them whether they'd seen anything, but I didn't tell them what it was about."

Joe stared at him for silent seconds. He strode across the floor and violently kicked the trash can.

"*Fuck!*"

Ethan startled, fingers twitching around the cup. He'd expected Joe to be furious if he found out about the stalker, but he had not anticipated the rage visibly burning through the man. A flame of hope shot through him and licked a treacherous path along his veins.

Does this mean he cares? Even a little?

"Why, Ethan? Tell me why," Joe said harshly. "Why haven't you talked to me about this when it's been going on right under my nose?"

"I—" Ethan swallowed. "It—it didn't concern you. And I wanted to take care of this myself. I'm a man, for fuck's sake!"

Joe gritted his teeth and glared at him.

"Men rape and kill other men every day."

Ethan felt blood drain from his face at Joe's stark words.

"And, just in case it escaped that moronic brain of yours, I actually happen to own this place," Joe continued hotly. "The place where this all started. As far as I see it, this concerns me one hundred and ten percent. So, tell me, Ethan. Why?"

Ethan briefly closed his eyes. He couldn't very well reveal to Joe the real reason he'd lied to him by omission.

Joe drew a breath in sharply.

"Is this because I refuse to *fuck* you?"

Oh God.

Ethan suddenly wished the floor would open up and swallow him.

❧

JOE'S ANGER REACHED BOILING POINT WHEN HE READ THE truth on Ethan's shocked face.

The little—

"I don't fucking believe it," Joe said, clenching his teeth so hard his jaw ached. "How could you put yourself at risk for such a stupid reason?"

Ethan blinked before narrowing his eyes.

"Well, excuse me for being a moron."

Joe stared.

I can't believe the stubborn prick is challenging me right now.

The thought of all the terrible things that could have happened to the young man glaring at him so daringly sent an icy chill down Joe's spine once more. He'd seen this kind of thing plenty times before, when he was still working the strip clubs in New York. Men and women who were relentlessly chased by clients who wanted to own them, body and soul. Most had escaped their stalkers unscathed. The few who hadn't almost always ended up in the hospital, violently raped and beaten to near death.

A stark truth had bolted through Joe when Ethan had told him about the anonymous notes he'd been getting at the club.

Although he refused to acknowledge what it was exactly he felt for Ethan, he couldn't—no, he *wouldn't* let anything happen to the cocky bartender who had wormed his way into his life and continued to frustrate the hell out of him nearly every single day since their first meeting.

That shocking realization had led Joe to one undeniable conclusion. Even if he had to lock Ethan up in a basement, he'd keep the young man safe until he figured out the identity of the man stalking him and gave the bastard a piece of his mind. Preferably with his fists.

CHAPTER FOUR

"Is there anything else you want to tell me before I decide what to do about this?"

Ethan stared at Joe. A strange expression had washed across the club owner's face mere seconds ago. He was still wondering what it was when Joe scowled, suspicion darkening his eyes.

"Ethan?"

Ethan stiffened.

Oh, crap. He's gonna be SO pissed.

"Well—," Ethan rubbed a hand across the back of his neck and lowered his gaze to the floor, "—he's also, er, left notes at my place."

Deafening silence filled the room. Ethan peeked up and swallowed hard.

Yup, fucking livid.

"What?" Joe said silkily, hands slowly fisting by his sides.

"And flowers," Ethan added meekly. "He started leaving flowers in the back alley."

"Flowers?" Joe repeated in a lifeless voice.

Ethan grimaced.

"To be fair, it was only ever a single rose at a time."

Joe inhaled deeply.

"So, let me get this straight. For the last three months, this guy's been leaving you notes at the club. He found out where you live and has been leaving you notes at your apartment, too. And, now, you're telling me he's been giving you *fucking* flowers?"

"Er, like I said, only the one rose—"

"I don't care if the guy's wooing you with a goddamn forest full of blooms, Ethan!" Joe snarled.

He marched toward Ethan, took the cup from Ethan's grasp, and slammed it down on the coffee table.

Ethan gasped when Joe grabbed the front of his shirt and hauled him to his feet.

"Here's how we're going to do things from now on," Joe said icily. "You're going to tell me the next time you get one of these notes or—*flowers*! We're going to inform the rest of the staff about this, so they can keep a lookout for this jerk. And I'm going to install cameras everywhere in the club."

Ethan gulped. Warmth spread across his chest where Joe's fingers twisted in his shirt. He'd never been this close to the club owner before.

"And another thing," Joe said harshly, hazel eyes boring into Ethan's, seemingly oblivious to the slow ache building in Ethan's groin. "We're now officially dating."

All thoughts of how good Joe smelled up close and

the delicious heat radiating off the hard body so close to his fled Ethan's mind in a flash.

"What—*what* did you just say?!" Ethan stammered between numb lips.

"You heard me right the first time," Joe said frostily. He tugged Ethan closer. "We're going to play pretend lovers until we flush out this bastard."

Ethan's heart slammed against his ribs as he found himself suddenly pressed against Joe's body.

Oh God.

Ethan swallowed hard.

"Um, how pretend are we talking here?"

Joe blinked slowly. He looked up at the ceiling and closed his eyes.

"Jesus, give me *fucking* strength."

Ethan watched Joe's Adam's apple bob a couple of inches from his nose. The urge to stick out his tongue and lick it washed over him in the next instant. He peeked up at the man scowling at him and decided that now was not the time to push his luck.

JOE WATCHED ETHAN BROODINGLY FROM THE TOP OF THE steps leading to the sunken floor, one shoulder propped against the wall and a Scotch in hand. Despite the incident in the alley, Ethan had insisted on working his shift. He stood behind the bar, full of his usual smiles and quick banter while he served the club's patrons.

"Christ, you wouldn't think there was anything wrong, looking at him," Joe muttered.

"You talking to yourself, Joe?"

Joe turned at the familiar voice. A tall man with dark hair and gray eyes stood grinning at him. A wave of warmth and affection washed through Joe as he studied his best friend.

That he and Cam Sorvino had found each other again twenty years after they ran away together from the children's home where they'd spent the best part of their early teens was both a miracle and a blessing.

"Cam." Joe gave Cam a quick hug and dipped his chin at the blue-eyed man beside him. "Good to see you, Gabe. It's been a while."

Gabe Anderson nodded and murmured a quiet greeting.

Joe still found it hard to believe that Cam had hooked up with the gorgeous design consultant from Damon & Tucker, breaking his lifelong tradition of one-night stands and shelving his previous abhorrence of relationships. Yet Joe could see why the two of them made such a good pair. They complemented each other perfectly, Cam's hard personality moderated by Gabe's quieter temperament. And the sexual chemistry between them was so obvious a blind man could see it, as was the fact that they clearly cherished one another.

Joe wondered whether Cam and Gabe realized yet that this was more than a casual connection. That the bonds between them were fast growing into love. He grinned.

"What's that smile for?" Cam said, puzzled.

"Nothing." Joe signaled one of the waiters and ordered a double Scotch for each man.

"Thanks," Gabe said. He linked his fingers through Cam's.

Cam smiled at his lover before cocking an eyebrow at Joe.

"Catch you later?"

Joe dipped his chin.

"Sure."

The pair headed down the steps, Cam hovering over Gabe as heads turned their way.

Joe shook his head.

Like a fucking mother hen.

He turned his attention to the crowd of men filling *Saron*. Though it was a Tuesday night, the club was buzzing. Tension wound through Joe as he scanned the sea of shadowy faces.

Is he here? Is he watching Ethan right now?

He glanced at the other bartenders working the counter. They were sticking close to Ethan, their protective stance evident only to him and the rest of the staff.

They'd all been shocked when Joe had gathered them before *Saron* opened its doors that evening and told them about what had been going on with Ethan. Even Kiba the doorman had scolded the bartender, while Michelle the singer called him several unsavory names.

Though the high color in Ethan's cheeks had told Joe he'd been overwhelmed by their concern and just a tad embarrassed at the fuss, the hint of vulnerability in the depths of Ethan's normally carefree eyes had sent a sharp pain shooting through Joe. He'd pushed the feeling down into the cold depths of his heart, unwilling to admit its existence.

Anger twisted Joe's gut as his gaze swept the club floor once more. It was time for Act One.

Let's show this asshole just who he's gonna have to deal with from now on.

CHAPTER FIVE

"Here you go." Ethan placed the cocktail on the counter and slid it toward the man who'd ordered it. "Enjoy," he added with a smile.

The guy nodded and twisted on his barstool, stirring the drink with a cocktail stick while he conversed with his friends.

Ethan ruled him out as his stalker, took the next order, and turned to grab a bottle of gin from the shelf behind the bar.

One of the other bartenders sidled up to him and reached for the Courvoisier.

"How're you holding up, kiddo?"

Ethan bit back a sigh and looked at the handsome Japanese man with the retro black-rimmed specs studying him with concern in his eyes.

"Akihito, I swear to God, if you ask me that question one more time, I'm gonna floor you. And you're, like, two years older than me."

Akihito frowned and tut-tutted.

"You can bitch all you want, sweet cheeks, but I ain't letting you out of my sight." He twisted away and flashed a bright smile at the man who'd ordered the Sidecar.

Ethan shook his head slightly while he mixed a G & T. Movement to the left caught his gaze when he turned back to hand the drink to the patron. Joe was headed for the bar, his eyes locked on Ethan. The expression on the club owner's face sent a sudden shiver down Ethan's spine.

Oh, fuck. Now what?

Surprise darted through Ethan when Joe came around the counter and opened the hatch. He dropped it, closed the distance to Ethan in half a dozen steps, grabbed him by the waist, and kissed him hard.

Ethan froze and stared up blankly into Joe's stormy gaze while the latter pressed his hot lips against his own, his stubble grazing Ethan's chin.

Shocked gasps echoed along the counter. The noise level in the club dropped fractionally before rising to fever pitch, the entire room reeling as word spread.

Intuition flashed through Ethan.

Though it hurt to acknowledge it, he understood Joe's intent. Still, he wasn't about to let their first kiss be born out of anger.

Ethan ignored Joe's bruising touch, lifted his hands to Joe's face, and melted against him.

Joe blinked when Ethan softened below him, his fingers achingly gentle where they lay on Joe's cheeks, his long eyelashes fluttering against his face as he closed his dazzling green eyes. Ethan let out a breathy moan.

Heat shot through Joe and arrowed straight to his groin at the sensuous sound. His dick twitched and stiffened.

Shit.

Joe loosened his grip on Ethan's waist. His anger faded as he explored the full lips beneath his, curiously molding them with his own, knowing he was playing with fire yet unable to stop himself.

Joe probed the soft mouth beneath his with his tongue.

Ethan shuddered and parted his lips, eyes blinking open for a moment. The hunger in the emerald depths sent a torrid wave of lust surging through Joe. He cradled Ethan's face and swooped inside the opening, his tongue invading the dark, hot space, caressing, exploring.

Unheeding of the dozens of stares focused on them and the shocked murmurs spreading across the club, Joe plundered Ethan's mouth, need a hot spring coiling tightly through him, twisting his belly and hardening his cock.

Ethan's tongue met his a heartbeat later.

The bolt of electricity that flashed through Joe almost made him groan out loud. From the way Ethan twitched and arched against him, Joe knew the bartender was also experiencing the same shocking sensation.

Joe pressed his thigh between Ethan's legs, dropped one hand to Ethan's tight butt cheeks, and deepened the kiss.

Ethan moaned and shuddered, his body dissolving against Joe's, his hands dropping from Joe's face to grip Joe's shoulders for support, his erection pushing sweetly against Joe's hard-on.

A wolf whistle reached Joe dimly through the red haze of pleasure flooding him from where his tongue danced with Ethan's. He recognized Cam's laughter and could imagine Gabe groaning in sheer embarrassment at his lover's crass behavior.

Had his own hands not been full of the insanely sexy man he was currently kissing, Joe would have shoved a middle finger at his best friend. It was with reluctance that Joe lifted his mouth off Ethan's a moment later. He didn't think he'd be able to stop if he carried on for much longer.

Ethan panted below him, chest rising and falling with his labored breathing, his full lips swollen and red from Joe's kiss. He blinked up at Joe, his green eyes dark with passion.

Joe bit back a groan at the erotic picture of an aroused Ethan, his dick throbbing uncomfortably against the zipper of his pants.

"That was—" Ethan mumbled.

"Act One," Joe said, his words coming out harsher than he'd intended.

Ethan stiffened against him, desire slowly fading

from his eyes.

"Right," he muttered, his tone bitter.

⚘

ETHAN FINISHED DRYING THE LAST GLASS AND PLACED IT on the rack. It was two in the morning and the club was empty, bar Akihito and Kiba. Though it wasn't his turn to clean up, Ethan had been reluctant to return to his apartment and had stayed back to help. Besides, he was still reeling from his first kiss with Joe. He'd found his fingers rising unconsciously to his mouth several times for the rest of that night, the heated tingle of Joe's touch still evident on his lips.

Despite having spent the best part of ten minutes explaining the reason behind Joe's behavior to a frankly intrigued Akihito and Kiba, the bartender and the doorman continued to watch Ethan with indulgent expressions, as if they knew something he didn't know.

This did nothing to calm Ethan's racing heart and fevered imagination.

The reason for his current predicament strolled into the bar.

Joe shrugged his jacket on and paused by the mahogany counter, his hazel gaze locking on Ethan.

"You about done?"

Ethan blinked, nonplussed.

"What?"

Joe sighed. "I'm asking if you're ready to go."

"Go where?" Ethan said suspiciously.

Kiba grunted.

"He's saying he wants to walk you home, kid."

"Thank you, Kiba," Joe murmured, his eyes mocking as he continued staring at Ethan.

"Ay-ay-ay, how romantic!" Akihito squealed, hands rising dramatically to his cheeks.

Ethan narrowed his eyes at the bartender.

"One of these days, I'm gonna video you acting all camp and send it to your wife."

Akihito grinned, unabashed.

"She loves me, warts and all, sweet cheeks. Nothing you do will ever change that."

Ethan sighed, his pulse starting a steady, rising beat as he studied Joe. He knew refusing the club owner would only end in an argument. And there was no denying that the incident in the alley still sent shivers through Ethan's body.

"Give me a couple of minutes."

Joe was waiting for Ethan outside the staff changing room when he came out.

Ethan looked over his shoulder toward the silent club.

"Where are Kiba and Akihito?"

"They locked up and left. Come, we'll go out this way."

Joe turned and led Ethan through the private door to his apartment. Beyond the small lobby and spiral stairs was another exit opening onto a side alley. They headed north, the sound of traffic from the main Shinjuku strip slowly fading behind them.

Although Ethan was acutely conscious of Joe beside him as they navigated the roads toward his apartment building, he found the silence between them strangely comforting.

It wasn't long before they reached his street.

Ethan stopped in front of his building and looked at Joe, feeling awkward for the first time since they stepped out of *Saron*.

"Well, this is—"

"I'm paying you too much," Joe said bluntly. He stared at the pleasant neighborhood around them before studying Ethan's building with narrowed eyes. "I knew you lived in Bunkyo, but I wasn't expecting this."

Ethan gazed at him, intrigued.

"What were you expecting?"

Joe frowned.

"Some crappy studio flat with shared facilities. This place looks like it's serviced."

Irritation replaced Ethan's curiosity. He scowled.

"Sometimes, the shit that comes out of your mouth really pisses me off. And you're right. It is."

Ethan removed his key card from his back pocket, slipped it in the door, and pushed it open.

Lights came on, illuminating the empty lobby and the rows of letterboxes to the left.

"Thanks for walking me home," Ethan said coolly over his shoulder. "I'll—"

"I'm coming in," Joe said behind him.

CHAPTER SIX

ETHAN BLINKED RAPIDLY WHEN JOE CROWDED HIM against the half-open door.

"Why?"

Joe glowered.

"This asshole nearly chased you in that alley tonight and he's been sending you notes to this place. I want to check your apartment."

Ethan swallowed, his pulse accelerating at Joe's proximity despite his annoyance at the carefully orchestrated charade they were now engaged in.

God, he smells good.

Joe hustled him inside the lobby and inspected the letterboxes as the door swung closed behind them.

"Which one's yours?"

Ethan hesitated. "Three-oh-one."

Joe looked at him pointedly. Ethan sighed and handed him the key card.

Joe opened the letterbox. It was empty. He frowned.

"What kind of stuff does he normally send his notes in?"

"White envelopes. About the size of a greeting card."

Joe scanned the clean lines of the lobby, suspicion creasing his brow.

"You sure it's not your mailman?"

Ethan narrowed his eyes.

"My *mailman* is a fifty-five-year old lady with arthritis."

"Oh." Joe watched him for a silent moment. "Lead the way."

JOE STUDIED THE SWEET CURVES OF ETHAN'S BUTT AS the bartender climbed the stairs ahead of him.

The memory of the kiss they'd shared earlier that night still burned through him. Joe had expected that making out with Ethan would be hot, but the reality of it had utterly stunned him. He still regretted the words he'd spoken following the kiss, the ones he'd uttered to make it clear to Ethan that this was all just an act to flush out his unwanted admirer. Deep down inside, Joe knew he'd also said those words to remind himself that he needed to keep his distance from Ethan.

Despite the bartender's cool behavior for the rest of that evening, Joe had still insisted on walking Ethan home, his concern about the stalker situation unabated.

Although Joe had enjoyed the companionable silence they'd shared as they strolled to the bartender's home, he had only intended to make sure Ethan got to his apartment building okay. One look at the place and the exclusive neighborhood it was set in had sent a bolt of intense curiosity through Joe.

Who the hell is this kid?

"Joe," Ethan said quietly as they negotiated a landing.

"Yeah?"

"Quit staring at my ass."

Joe blinked.

"What makes you think I'm staring at your ass?"

"'Cause I can feel your eyes boring a hole into it."

"You mean, besides the other hole?"

Ethan cursed and mumbled something that sounded like, "Irritating fucker," above him.

Joe grinned. He was glad to see Ethan back to his normal self.

The bartender stopped on the third landing and headed left down the corridor. He paused in front of the door to his apartment and put his hand out.

"My key card."

Joe ignored him, slipped the plastic strip in the lock, and twisted the handle. Lights came on as he entered the apartment ahead of Ethan.

Joe stopped and stared at the open-plan living area, the dark oak wood floor, and the sleek lines of chic furniture dotting the place. He frowned at Ethan over his shoulder.

"Care to tell me how you can afford this on the wage I'm paying you?"

"I came into some inheritance money and invested

it wisely," Ethan said, deadpan. He shrugged his jacket off and barged past Joe.

Irritation flashed through Joe. He could spot a barefaced lie from a mile away. That Ethan was holding back on telling him the truth again made his gut twist with anger. He marched after Ethan, grabbed his arm, and spun him around.

"You're lying to me, Ethan," Joe said silkily. "And you should know by now, I don't like liars."

Ethan's gaze dropped to where Joe's hand was wrapped around his right biceps. The fury in his green eyes when he looked up made Joe blink in surprise.

"If anyone is lying, it's you," Ethan said harshly.

Joe slowly released his hold on the bartender.

"And exactly what do you mean by that?"

"You fucking well know what I'm talking about!"

Ethan dropped his jacket on a sofa chair and twisted on his heels to face Joe.

"Why do you still go there? To *Le Secret*? What kind of hold does that—that *woman* have on you that you would sell yourself for her when you clearly don't need the money?"

Joe stilled.

"That's none of your business," he said coldly.

"Oh, yeah? Well, it's none of *your* business how I can afford this place either!" Ethan spat.

Joe clenched his jaw as he stared at the gorgeous, irate man before him.

"I owe Eveline my life."

Ethan blinked, shock replacing the anger on his face.

"What?" he mumbled.

Joe raked a hand through his hair.

"I would be long dead by now if Eveline hadn't rescued me from the hellhole I was living in back in New York."

Ethan paled.

"Is she blackmailing you?"

"No." Joe scowled. "That's all I'm gonna say on the subject, so don't push me, Ethan."

ETHAN'S HEART THUNDERED INSIDE HIS CHEST AS JOE strode past him, still reeling from the club owner's unexpected confession.

Joe checked the apartment and returned to the living area a moment later.

"Everything looks okay," he said gruffly.

Ethan nodded mutely.

"I'll come pick you up tomorrow before your shift," Joe said.

He dropped Ethan's key card on the coffee table and headed for the door.

"You don't need to do that," Ethan murmured, walking slowly after him.

Joe froze with his hand on the door handle. He turned, grabbed Ethan's arm, and pushed him against the hallway wall.

Ethan gasped when Joe trapped his wrists above his head with his powerful hands and pressed his tall, hard body against him.

"What the—"

Joe swooped and swallowed the rest of Ethan's words with his lips, his kiss sending electricity surging through Ethan, his hot tongue masterfully invading Ethan's mouth.

Ethan moaned and arched, hips flexing against the steely leg wedged between his thighs. Joe pushed back, his erection digging into Ethan's stomach. He kept Ethan's wrists trapped with one hand and dropped the other to Ethan's groin.

Fire licked Ethan when Joe ran a finger across his throbbing cock.

"*Oh!*"

Ethan felt Joe grin against his lips. Then, his entire world narrowed in on the sound of a zipper opening and the draft of air that washed across his lower abdomen.

Ethan groaned with pleasure as Joe dipped his hand inside his briefs and palmed his aching cock. He wrenched his mouth from Joe's kiss and dropped his head back against the wall as the latter started stroking him with delicious, slow movements of his wrist.

"Oh God."

"You like that?" Joe whispered teasingly in his left ear, his breath sending a shiver of need down Ethan's spine.

Ethan bit his lower lip.

"*Yes!*"

"Good," Joe murmured. He dropped hot kisses against Ethan's neck, his hand working him faster and faster.

Ethan matched Joe's rhythm with his own hips, thrusting into the fingers pleasuring him, unable to halt the gasps and moans leaving his throat. The first wave of his climax gathered at the base of his spine and deep inside his belly a moment later.

"*Oh Jesus!*" Ethan closed his eyes, his ass clenching tight and his entire body stiffening in anticipation of the intense orgasm.

Joe's hand froze on his cock.

Ethan blinked dazedly and looked up at him. Confusion clouded his pleasure-dazed brain when he registered Joe's cool expression.

"This is your punishment for lying to me," Joe said stonily.

He let go of him so suddenly, Ethan nearly collapsed to the floor.

Ethan pressed his back against the wall, knees trembling and cock throbbing. Shock turned to anger when he realized he'd just been masterfully played.

"You fucking asshole," Ethan hissed.

Joe's gaze dropped to Ethan's stiff dick.

"That looks kinda painful. I'd take care of it if I were you."

He turned and headed out of the apartment. The door closed loudly in the deafening silence.

Rage flooded Ethan. He slipped his aching cock inside his pants, opened the door, and glared at Joe's back as the latter strolled toward the stairs.

"*You fucking asshole!*"

Joe stopped and arched an eyebrow at him over his shoulder.

"I'll pick you up at five. Be ready."

CHAPTER SEVEN

Ethan was still fuming two days later. He scowled across the mahogany counter he was polishing to where Joe was supervising the final camera installation by the security company he'd hired.

"What's wrong with you?" Akihito muttered.

"Nothing," Ethan growled.

Akihito's gaze swung from Ethan to Joe and back again.

"Are you guys having a lovers' spat?"

Fury and shame twisted Ethan's stomach in equal measure as he thought of that night at his apartment. Despite his anger at what Joe had done to him, Ethan hadn't been able to stop himself from jerking off to the hot image of that bastard giving him a hand job, his body so inflamed that it had taken three toe-curling orgasms for his throbbing dick to finally stop hurting.

"We are *not* lovers," Ethan said between gritted teeth. "I wouldn't let that fucker near me if he were the last man alive."

"Oh."

"In fact, that douche bag can kiss my ass if he thinks I'm ever gonna let him touch me again."

Akihito sucked air between his teeth.

"*Ooh.* So, there's been touching—"

"I hope his dick rots and falls off."

Akihito winced. "Okay, as a man, I think that's going a bit too far."

&

JOE SIGHED WHEN HE CAUGHT SIGHT OF ETHAN'S reflection in the mirror on the wall opposite him.

The bartender was glaring at him, jaw clenched while he spoke in a low voice to Akihito.

Joe didn't have to be a genius to figure out the content of their conversation. Leaving Ethan two nights ago had been one of the hardest things Joe had ever done in his adult life. He had known he was playing with fire when he'd touched Ethan, but the sight of the aroused, moaning young man about to come apart in his arms had struck Joe like a bucket of icy water, drenching his own arousal and freezing his hand on Ethan's gorgeously flushed cock.

In that moment, Joe had known there would be no going back if he witnessed Ethan's orgasm. He would have taken Ethan there and then against that wall, repeatedly thrusting his throbbing dick into Ethan's tight ass, driving them both wild with pleasure while he swallowed Ethan's cries and moans with his mouth.

It would have been the best sex Joe would ever have had—that, he was certain of.

It would also have been very wrong.

Joe knew what Ethan wanted. And he couldn't give it to him.

"All done, Mr. Cavendish," said the camera guy. He climbed down the stepladder and picked up the tablet on the table next to them. He tapped out a password and showed the screen to Joe. "This should work even if someone cuts the power. You can set it up on your computer and phone, too."

Grim satisfaction coursed through Joe as he observed the feeds from the cameras he'd had placed around the club.

There's no way this asshole's gonna get close to this place without us catching him in the act now.

Motion on one of the feeds caught his gaze.

Ethan was shoving his middle finger at the camera located on the wall behind the bar, a scowl darkening his features.

"Um," the security guy murmured awkwardly.

Joe chuckled, amused despite himself.

"It's all right," he told the bemused man. "His boyfriend's been giving him a hard time."

THE LETTER ARRIVED WITH THE NEXT MORNING'S MAIL. Joe paused inside the foyer, his fingers stilling on the white envelope. It was about the size Ethan had mentioned the notes the stalker sent to him came in.

Joe's name and the club's address were scrawled across it in angry black handwriting.

Joe's heart stuttered when he opened it and saw the contents. Tucked inside the fold of a card were pictures of Ethan.

They'd been taken while Ethan was evidently oblivious that he was being captured on camera. There were shots of him drinking coffee at a Starbucks, eating lunch, walking down the street, going for a run, and even working out at a gym, the lens focusing on his sweat-slicked face and body.

The last two images sent ice dancing along Joe's veins.

They'd been Photoshopped and showed Ethan's face superimposed on the body of a man who had been tied to a bed and was getting his ass pumped by a giant dildo. In the second shot, he'd been forced onto his knees and was getting fucked by one man while another shoved his dick down his throat, his chin dribbling with cum.

Joe's pulse raced when he read the words on the card.

"Stay away from him or I will violate him and kill him."

Rage burned through Joe, so sudden and vicious he saw red. He twisted and punched the wooden paneling of the wall with his fist.

This fucker!

"What the hell are you doing?" someone said behind him.

Joe whipped around, his heart slamming against his ribs.

Ethan was standing in the club's doorway, a puzzled look on his face. His gaze dropped to Joe's hands.

"What's that?"

Joe crumpled the card and photographs and lowered his fisted hand by his side, fighting to control the dread and anger rushing through him.

"What are you doing here?" he said gruffly. "It's your day off."

"I forgot my gym card in the changing room." Suspicion slowly darkened the green eyes staring at Joe. Ethan's gaze dropped briefly to Joe's hand again. "What's going on?"

Joe remained silent.

Ethan's pupils flared.

"Wait, is that another letter?"

Joe hesitated.

"Yes," he finally admitted between clenched teeth.

Ethan narrowed his eyes. "Show it to me."

Joe frowned. "No."

Ethan drew a sharp breath in.

"Why the fuck not? It's addressed to me, isn't it?" He closed the distance between them and grabbed Joe's white-knuckled hand.

"No, it isn't." Joe clasped the bartender's wrist with his other hand and tugged. "Let go, Ethan!"

Ethan bared his teeth and fought him.

"Stop it!" Joe snarled. He pushed Ethan against the wall. "You *don't* want to see this!"

Ethan struggled against him. Joe cursed as the card and photographs slipped out of his hand and landed on the floor by their feet. Ethan lunged, grabbed the wrinkled sheets, and unfolded them before Joe could stop him. He froze, blood draining from his face as he scanned the message and images.

Joe's heart twisted painfully at the haunted expression that filled Ethan's eyes.

A shudder ran through Ethan. He leaned against the wall, the card and pictures fluttering out of his hands and falling to the floor, his eyes wide and staring blindly at Joe.

Alarm filled Joe when he registered Ethan's ragged breathing and trembling legs. He reached out and gently took the young man in his arms.

"It's okay," Joe said quietly. He dropped a kiss on the thick blond hair tickling his chin. "We're gonna find this bastard and stop him."

Ethan's body was rigid against Joe, his breaths coming harder and faster.

"I can't—*I can't breathe!*" he gasped.

Joe's pulse jumped when he looked into Ethan's ashen face and heard his labored pants. He grabbed Ethan's shoulders.

"Ethan, you're having a panic attack! Just calm down, okay!"

Ethan shook his head, his pupils wide, air wheezing past his lips.

Joe cursed. He cradled the young man's face and stared into his frightened eyes.

"Breathe," he ordered.

Joe swooped and took Ethan's mouth, pouring everything he had into the kiss, forcing Ethan to match his own breaths.

Ethan stiffened before shuddering against him. He parted his lips, his irregular gasps washing across Joe's tongue, his fingers biting into Joe's shoulders.

Joe didn't stop until Ethan's laborious breathing eased and the shivers racking his body finally stopped. He started lifting his mouth off Ethan's reluctantly.

Ethan shuddered again, his grasp tightening on Joe's flesh. For a moment, Joe thought the panic attack was gaining its grip on Ethan once more. Then Ethan softened and melted into Joe, passion overcoming his fear, his tongue lashing sensuously against Joe's as he demanded more from their kiss. Joe stiffened for an instant before responding, sucking and nibbling on Ethan's tongue. It was only when Ethan moaned under him that Joe finally let go of his lips.

Ethan blinked and stared up at him dazedly, his cheeks flushed and his mouth plump and rosy from Joe's kiss.

Joe swallowed a groan of need and dropped his forehead against Ethan's. "Better?" he said raggedly.

Ethan nodded shakily. His face sobered as he glanced at the pictures on the floor. "Shit," he muttered in a trembling voice.

"I'm calling the cops," Joe said in a hard voice.

Ethan hesitated before dipping his chin in agreement.

CHAPTER EIGHT

Ethan checked himself in the floor-length mirror in his bedroom for the tenth time, his heart drumming steadily against his ribs.

Two days had passed since he'd seen the awful pictures that had been delivered to *Saron* along with the threatening note addressed to Joe. Although the detectives who had come to the club promised they would look into the matter further, Ethan could tell from Joe's stormy expression that he didn't think it would be enough. That must have been why he'd suggested the mad plan about to unfold.

"What are you doing this Sunday?" Joe had asked gruffly after the detective and his partner left the club.

Ethan had shrugged, puzzled. Sunday was the one day the club was closed.

"Nothing in particular. Why?"

"We're going on a date."

Ethan had blinked. "What?"

"I said, we're going on a date," Joe had repeated, his hazel eyes glinting hotly as he stared at Ethan across the staff room. "Be ready by one."

Ethan had barely slept the night before, his fevered imagination coming up with all sorts of scenarios about what he and Joe would do on their date. Then, Ethan had recalled the cruel things Joe had done to him that night when he came to his apartment and the tender way he'd managed Ethan's first panic attack only a couple of days past.

The man is one fucking ornery contradiction.

Ethan sighed, decided his outfit would have to do, and headed out the door.

Joe was standing under the awning of the apartment building, head bowed as he read something on his cell, his back to the wall and his legs crossed. He was dressed in jeans, a crisp white shirt, and a camel-colored blazer.

Ethan's mouth went dry as he navigated the lobby. He slowed to a stop and watched Joe for a moment, his breath stilling in his throat. It wasn't every day he had a chance to properly look at the man he'd fallen in love with nearly a year ago without the bastard being aware of it.

Ethan's gaze skimmed Joe's rugged features and full lips before dropping to his large hands and the hard lines of his body, a slow ache building in his groin as he stared at Joe's denim-encased long legs.

That he'd been pressed against that incredible physique and kissed those delicious lips was something Ethan could still not quite believe.

Joe looked up then. His eyes flared when he saw Ethan standing behind the glass wall. He put his cell away.

Ethan swallowed and steeled himself before exiting the lobby and strolling over to Joe.

"Hey," he murmured self-consciously.

Joe's gaze skimmed Ethan from head to toe, appreciation darkening his hazel eyes as he took in Ethan's gray designer jeans, moss-colored T-shirt, and denim jacket.

"You scrub up nice."

"So do you," Ethan said. "For an old guy."

Joe sighed.

"I'm thirty-five."

Ethan grinned, shoulders dropping and body relaxing at their familiar banter. "So, what are we doing?"

"I thought we'd take a walk through the park in Chiyoda, maybe catch a movie in Ginza."

"Be still my beating heart," Ethan said deadpan.

Joe's lips twitched as they started down the road.

"After that, we're having dinner in Roppongi. I booked us a table at *Ryugin*."

Ethan's eyes widened at the mention of the Michelin-starred restaurant.

"Now you're talking."

❧

JOE LEANED AGAINST THE RAILING, THE NIGHT AIR FRESH against his face. He glanced at Ethan where he stood beside him, green gaze sweeping the majestic vista.

"I never tire of this view," the bartender murmured.

They were on the Sky Deck atop Mori Tower, the huge complex at the heart of Roppongi Hills. The city of Tokyo was spread out below and around them, a dazzling display of colorful lights stretching out as far as the eye could see, the noise from the distant traffic a background drone.

Joe smiled faintly at Ethan's admission. He was surprised at how much fun he'd had on their date. From their leisurely walk through the park to the cheesy chick flick Ethan had forced Joe to watch in revenge for his past misdeeds, to the amazing meal they'd just shared, Joe didn't think he'd enjoyed himself so much in someone else's company, bar Cam, before.

They left Roppongi a short while later and made their way back to Bunkyo, both of them dragging their feet while they chatted, neither wishing for their date to end. They reached Ethan's building far too fast for Joe's liking.

Ethan hesitated on the porch, his key card in hand, his expression telling Joe he was just as reluctant for them to part ways.

"Thanks for today," he said quietly. "It was a great idea to try to flush him out, but I don't think it worked."

Joe's pulse started a steady rising beat in his veins as he studied Ethan.

"We can try again."

Ethan's eyes flared at Joe's words. His gaze turned heavy-lidded and dropped to Joe's mouth.

"Sure," he murmured, his voice sultry.

Shit.

Joe grabbed Ethan's waist and pushed him against the glass exterior of the lobby. He wedged one leg between Ethan's thighs, angled Ethan's head with one hand, and pounced on his mouth.

Ethan's breathing turned ragged. His hands rose to clutch Joe's shoulders, his lips parting sweetly beneath Joe's mouth, letting him in. Joe accepted the invitation with an eager thrust of his tongue and was rewarded by the delicious shudder that ran through Ethan and the way he flexed his hips against his leg.

So fucking sexy.

Joe deepened the kiss, his cock swelling and throbbing against Ethan's belly, pleasure sparking through his entire body as Ethan's tongue danced with his, the bartender's breathy gasps and moans an erotic music that inflamed Joe's senses further.

A noise reached him dimly through the blood roaring in his ears. Joe blinked and caught movement in the reflection in the glass opposite him.

Someone stood staring at them from behind a bush across the road.

Joe stiffened. He wrenched his mouth from Ethan's and twisted on his heels.

The figure turned and ran.

"Get inside!" Joe shouted at Ethan over his shoulder as he gave chase.

The bartender nodded shakily, body rooted to the ground for a frozen moment before he slid his key card in the lock and stumbled inside the lobby.

Joe's angry gaze found the man sprinting along the walkway some fifty feet away.

Gotcha, you bastard!

He put his head down and accelerated, feet pounding the asphalt.

The man suddenly dove to the right and disappeared from view.

Joe's stomach twisted. He reached the spot where he'd last seen him and glimpsed a shadowy figure cutting across a small park. He vaulted over the railing and followed, his heart racing in his chest.

Shit, he's heading for the subway!

Joe cursed as Ethan's stalker dashed inside Sengoku Station moments later. The man jumped over the barriers and headed for the platform just as a train pulled up.

A group of rowdy, drunk men stepped off, their tottering legs bringing them straight into Joe's path when he leaped over the barriers in pursuit. He swore as he slipped and shoved through them, losing precious seconds.

Joe reached the train just as the doors closed. He punched the carriage with his fist as it started to move, his breaths coming hard and fast. He stepped back and scanned the bright interior with narrowed eyes. His pulse stuttered when he caught a glimpse of a tall, hooded figure watching him as the train picked up speed and disappeared down the track.

Ethan was waiting inside the brightly lit lobby of his apartment building when Joe retraced his steps. His face was pale, his hands clenching and unclenching by his sides. He opened the front door and stepped out, relief washing across his anxious features.

"Thank God. I was—"

"Pack a bag," Joe ordered curtly. "You're staying over at mine from now on."

CHAPTER NINE

Ethan finished brushing his teeth and spat in the sink, his eyes avoiding his flushed reflection in the mirror. He looked around the small bathroom, his pulse pounding steadily in his veins. Joe's grooming products lined a couple of narrow shelves and his bath towel was draped across the heated rails next to the shower.

The room smelled of Joe. In fact, Joe's entire flat smelled of him.

Ethan closed his eyes and dropped his forehead against the mirror as he recalled the possessive look in Joe's eyes and his commanding tone when he'd ordered Ethan to grab a bag and come stay at his place.

Though Ethan had wanted to protest that this was a step too far, even he had to concede that what had happened had unnerved him.

That the stalker had been so close to them, watching them as they shared an intimate kiss, sent another shudder through Ethan.

He splashed water on his face, dried himself on the guest towel Joe had given him, and exited the bathroom. Four steps brought him to the living area and the couch Joe was preparing for him.

"It's a bit lumpy, but I think you'll be okay," Joe said, dropping a pair of pillows on top of a blanket.

He'd changed into gray-checkered pajama bottoms and a dark blue T-shirt.

Ethan swallowed as he glanced at Joe's muscled arms.

"Thanks," he murmured with a nod.

An hour later and Ethan was still nowhere near falling asleep. He'd tossed and turned, his mind filled with everything that had happened that day—from the amazing date he and Joe had shared and their thrilling kiss, to the terror that had filled him when Joe had vanished into the night after Ethan's stalker.

The minutes had felt like hours as Ethan waited, stomach twisting while he glanced repeatedly at his cell, wondering whether to call the cops but knowing they wouldn't be able to do anything unless Joe caught the guy. Ethan's feet had taken him to the door several times, his entire body eager and straining to give chase. Frustration had gnawed at him when he'd realized he wouldn't be a match for the giant figure who'd been stalking him, however fit and strong he was. Panic had twisted through Ethan at the thought that Joe might not be able to fight his stalker off either.

Ethan wanted nothing more than for the man who'd filled his life with fear to be stopped. But he could never forgive himself if Joe got hurt in the process.

Ethan twisted on the couch again, the springs moving and digging into his hip. He stared at the open doorway of the dark bedroom ten feet away, sighed, and rolled onto his back.

Shadows suddenly shifted on his right. He looked around, alarmed, and saw Joe walk out of his bedroom.

"If I hear those goddamn springs creak one more time," Joe muttered as he crossed the floor to the couch.

Ethan stared up at him in the gloom. "What are you—"

Ethan's breath left his lips in a whoosh in the next instant, his sentence cut off mid flow as Joe lifted him in his arms and tossed him unceremoniously over his shoulder. Joe ignored Ethan's incoherent protests and headed back into his bedroom.

Ethan gasped when Joe dropped him on his bed and climbed in after him. Joe tucked Ethan's head in the crook of his right elbow, wrapped his left arm around Ethan's chest as he rolled him on his side to face the window, and nudged his knees behind Ethan's, spooning him.

Ethan's heart hammered in his chest, the sound so loud he wondered if Joe could hear it and feel it against his arm. The scent of the man holding him and the large body pressed so intimately against his overwhelmed his senses, robbing him of the ability to speak. Heat flooded Ethan's cheeks in the next instant.

"Joe?" he breathed.

"Yeah?" Joe muttered, the rumble of his voice vibrating against Ethan's back and sending a shiver down his spine.

Ethan swallowed.

"Is that a stick in your pants?"

Joe sighed.

"Shut up and sleep, you little cocktease."

Ethan stifled a groan.

Sure, like that's gonna happen with your dick against my ass.

❧

JOE BLINKED GROGGILY.

Soft light bathed his bedroom, the curtains at the windows muting the sun's rays to an orange glow. He rubbed a hand across his face where he lay on his back and glanced at his watch.

It was eight in the morning.

Joe became aware of a weight pressing down on him and looked south. His breath caught in his throat.

Ethan was sleeping with his head tucked against Joe's chest, his right arm flung carelessly across Joe's body while his right leg rode high across Joe's thighs. Joe's pulse picked up as he stared at the bartender's gorgeous face. Ethan's long eyelashes rested against his creamy skin, the cocky mouth that usually challenged Joe relaxed in sleep and parted on soft, slow breaths.

Shit, he's even sexy when he's out cold.

Joe carefully folded his arms behind his head and settled down to watch Ethan sleep, a warm feeling slowly filling his chest as he gazed at the blond head moving gently with each rise and fall of his rib cage. He refused to analyze the emotion yet again, unwilling to give it a name, knowing that doing so would jeopardize the walls he'd built around his heart.

❧

ETHAN STIRRED, HIS MIND FUZZY WITH SLEEP. HE BURIED his face in the pillow and was snuggling into it when he realized it was hard, warm, and very much alive. He stiffened, his eyes slamming open. Ethan looked up and locked gaze with Joe where the latter lay watching him with an amused expression.

Ethan opened and closed his mouth soundlessly, mortification rendering him speechless when he registered the wanton way he was sprawled across Joe's body.

"Sleep well?" Joe drawled.

Ethan cleared his throat and nodded before carefully rolling off him.

Joe's arms snaked around Ethan's waist.

"Where do you think you're going?"

He tugged. Ethan gasped when he suddenly found himself completely on top of Joe.

Oh God.

Heat shot through Ethan at the feel of all the lines and angles of Joe's hard body pressed against him.

Joe grinned and brought his head up. Air locked in Ethan's throat when Joe stopped an inch from his mouth, his breaths sending tingles through Ethan as they washed across his lips, the expression in his hazel eyes taunting Ethan. Daring him. Ethan moaned and leaned down to press his mouth against Joe's.

A loud rumble erupted from somewhere between them.

Joe blinked before bursting out laughing.

"Shit." Ethan closed his eyes briefly and groaned, embarrassed at his stomach's untimely interruption. Joe's body shook beneath him as he chortled. "It's not funny," Ethan muttered. He pushed up to straddle Joe.

The new position stopped Joe short. His eyes darkened as he watched Ethan above him. He sat up, one hand rising to Ethan's back to pull him in, need flashing across his face as he brought his mouth up to kiss Ethan.

Another rumble boomed from the pit of Ethan's stomach.

He covered his face with his hands. "For fuck's sake."

Joe collapsed against him, his head dropping against Ethan's chest, his laughter echoing around the bedroom.

CHAPTER TEN

Ethan whistled a tune under his breath as he stirred the cocktail, the sound drowned by the music coming from the band playing on the stage at the far end of the club.

"Something good happen?" Akihito said, cocking an eyebrow.

Ethan smiled faintly. "You could say that."

Ethan's gaze flicked to where Joe sat talking with Cam and Gabe at a table some twenty feet away. Warmth filled him when he thought of the day they'd just shared.

After mercilessly teasing him that morning, Joe had made breakfast and served it on the tiny balcony overlooking the side alley next to *Saron*. They'd sat and eaten leisurely for the next few hours, their conversation so easy and flowing that Ethan's heart ached.

He would happily spend every morning like that with Joe for the rest of his life.

They'd moved to the club in the afternoon, Joe working away at his laptop and making phone calls while Ethan prepped things for that evening. He'd almost not wanted *Saron*'s doors to open, wishing he could prolong these precious moments with the man he loved.

The phone behind the bar rang, bringing Ethan back to the present. Akihito took the call while Ethan and the third bartender continued serving the club's patrons.

"Hey, you mind taking the delivery that just turned up?" Akihito called out to Ethan as he placed the phone back in its cradle. "The company's usual driver called in sick today. They just sent another guy with our stock. He's out back."

"Sure." Ethan finished an order, walked out from behind the counter, and headed to the rear of the club.

His cell vibrated as he crossed the kitchen and reached the door opening onto the rear alley. Ethan smiled when he saw the caller ID, turned the key in the lock, and grabbed the handle while he took the call.

"Hi, Sadie."

"Hey, Ethan," his aunt greeted him brightly. "Just calling to see how you're doing, hon."

"I'm great, thanks," Ethan said warmly as the night air washed over him. "What are you and Bob up to?"

He stepped out into the alley, saw the taillights of a truck parked to the left, and turned to look for the driver.

Fire exploded through Ethan's entire body from a spot on his chest, every single one of his muscles locking into painful spasm. Ethan's mouth opened on a silent cry of agony while his widening eyes took in the figure who'd tasered him. Something hard struck the side of his head in the next instant.

Consciousness fled as darkness claimed him.

❦

AN UNEASY FEELING SUDDENLY STIRRED INSIDE JOE. HE looked toward the bar.

"Hey, everything okay?" Cam said across from him. His best friend frowned faintly. "You've been kinda distracted all evening."

"Yeah, I'm just—" Joe started to say.

The rest of the words died on his lips. He stiffened when he registered the figures behind the counter.

Ethan wasn't there.

Joe rose and strode across the club, alarm rushing through him.

"Joe?" Cam called out behind him.

Joe ignored him, closing the distance to the bar in rapid, long steps.

He's probably in the restroom.

Joe's pulse thrummed wildly while he leaned across the mahogany counter, hoping with all his heart that was where Ethan had gone.

"Hey, Aki! Where's Ethan?" he called out to Akihito.

The bartender blinked at Joe's tense tone. "He went out back to get a delivery."

Joe's stomach twisted. "At *this* time of the night?"

Akihito grimaced. "Yeah, I thought it was strange too but—"

Joe whirled around and headed briskly toward the back of the club, the rest of Akihito's words swallowed by the noise of the crowd.

Please, God, let him be okay!

He couldn't explain the suffocating feeling filling his chest. The only thing he was sure of was what his instincts were telling him; something was wrong and whatever it was had everything to do with the man he very much feared he was already half in love with.

Joe's worst fears were confirmed when he found the back door ajar and the alley vacant except for a parked truck. He dashed around the vehicle, yanked the driver's door open, and climbed up to peer into the cabin and the cargo bay at the rear.

They were empty bar some crates.

Acid churned Joe's stomach as he jumped back down and ran into the middle of the passage. He raised white-knuckled hands to the sides of his head, his frantic gaze searching the shadows in both directions and finding nothing, terror nearly driving him to his knees.

Joe cursed as he suddenly recalled something. He took out his cell with trembling fingers and was bringing up the security feeds from the club's cameras when a faint sound reached his ears. He looked around and spotted Ethan's cell on the ground some fifteen feet to the east.

Joe stumbled toward the phone and picked it up. A

woman's panicked shouts reached him as he brought it to his ear.

"Who is this?" he barked, finger swiping across the screen of his own cell as he searched for the feed from the camera above the back door.

"I'm Sadie! Sadie Skye, Ethan's aunt!" the woman cried. "Who are you? Where's Ethan?! I was talking to him just now and—"

Joe froze when the feed finally came up on his cell, the woman's frightened words fading to a distant, dull roar. He bolted in the direction where he'd seen a man carry an unmoving Ethan.

"Sadie, my name is Joe Cavendish! I'm Ethan's boss! I'll call you back!"

Joe dropped the cell phones in his pockets and put his head down, his heart slamming erratically against his ribs. There was no time to call the cops.

He reached the crossroad at the end of the alley and slid to a stop, his gaze swinging north and south. A metallic noise came from somewhere to his left.

Joe turned and sprinted toward the sound. Voices called out to him from the direction of the club. He ignored them and accelerated.

A cat darted out of a side passage forty feet ahead and to the left. It hissed and arched its back as it stared at something in the darkness from where it'd come from before slinking away into the night.

Joe skidded around the corner seconds later.

He froze to a standstill, his feet rooted to the ground for a timeless moment. His heart stuttered in his chest as his entire world tilted to a stop.

A man straddled Ethan's body in the middle of the filthy passage, one hand locked around the bartender's throat, choking him while the latter struggled weakly beneath him. The man briskly worked his own erection with his other hand, his hips grinding against Ethan's clothed groin.

Redness filled Joe's vision. He snarled and bolted up the alley.

Ethan's attacker started to turn at the sound of Joe's footsteps. A grunt of surprise left him when Joe tackled him violently to the ground. They landed in a mess of tangled limbs, their breaths loud and harsh.

The man recovered faster than Joe had expected.

Joe blocked the knee swinging up toward his head and saw a taser coming at him from the corner of his eyes. He knocked it out of his assailant's hand with a growl and wrestled the man onto his back while the weapon skittered under a dumpster.

Joe's vision blurred as he yanked Ethan's stalker by the front of his shirt and repeatedly drove his fist into the man's face, grunts of rage leaving his lips. He didn't stop when he heard voices shouting out behind him. Didn't stop when they called out his name in alarm. Didn't stop until someone grabbed his wrist in an iron grip.

"Joe, you're gonna kill him!" Cam barked.

Joe blinked. Shudders racked his body as he stared down at Ethan's attacker, his arm straining rigidly in Cam's hold, dying to strike the man beneath him again.

The stranger's face was a bloodied pulp, his features

unrecognizable, his eyes swollen to glazed slits that looked at him unseeingly.

Joe moved off the stunned figure and sat down hard on the ground, his chest heaving with his ragged breathing while his hands dropped limply against his thighs. Blood pounded in his ears as he looked over his shoulder to where Gabe cradled Ethan's head in his lap. A visibly shaken Akihito was on his cell behind them, his face pale as he gave the cops directions to the alley.

Ethan started to come around. Air wheezed in and out of his lips as he coughed and tried to breathe through his swollen windpipe, the fingermarks around his neck livid in the pale light washing across the passage. His eyes widened when he registered his unconscious attacker and Joe's bleeding knuckles. A choked noise escaped him. His face crumpled.

Joe moved. He rose, stumbled unsteadily across the alley, and dropped by Ethan's side. He took Ethan from Gabe's arms and cradled his face to his body, rocking him gently while the latter shivered and shook against him. Wetness soaked Joe's chest. His heart shattered in a million pieces as Ethan's tears slowly stained his shirt.

CHAPTER ELEVEN

Ethan sighed and stared at the expensive bottle of champagne in his hand.

I should pop the cork and drink the whole damn thing.

A wry grin tugged at Ethan's lips at that thought. The smile faded almost immediately.

Two weeks had passed since that awful night when he was attacked by his stalker at the back of *Saron*. Two weeks during which he and Joe had had to give depositions at the Criminal Investigation Bureau. Two weeks during which the cops had uncovered disturbing evidence in the stalker's apartment, evidence that suggested he'd stalked and possibly attacked—or even worse, killed—other men in the past.

The guy had turned out to be a deliveryman for one of the beverage companies that supplied *Saron* and other clubs and bars across Tokyo. The detectives in charge of Ethan's case told him they'd started looking into unexplained disappearances of staff and patrons at all the places the company had delivered to since his stalker joined their payroll eight years ago.

As to the night Ethan had gotten attacked, it was sheer luck the stalker had been counting on when he faked the call from the company. Had Akihito or the third bartender come to the back door, the man would have abandoned his plans and returned another day.

Ethan had finally had to admit to his aunt what had been going on, although he'd brushed over the worst details. She'd wanted to get a flight to Tokyo straightaway to come see him. The only way he'd managed to dissuade her from doing so was to tell her that Joe was looking after him.

Which he was. Kind of.

Ethan stifled another sigh, placed the bottle of champagne back on the shelf, and poured himself a Scotch instead. He stared in the mirror behind the bar and touched his neck gingerly.

The bruises had nearly faded, as had the hoarseness of his voice following his near strangulation.

"I've sacked staff for less," someone said tartly.

Ethan spun around and stared at the stunning blonde eyeing him coolly from above the top of her sunglasses at the entrance to the club. She tucked the frames on her head and headed down the steps toward him, her red Manolo Blahnik heels striking the wooden floor leisurely while her white Chanel dress hugged her slender curves, a Prada purse tucked elegantly under one arm.

Recognition flashed through Ethan. He narrowed his eyes.

"We're not open yet," he said, his tone harsher than he'd intended.

The blonde ignored him and pulled herself smoothly onto a barstool.

"Pour me one, will you?" she drawled, indicating his glass of Scotch with a head tilt.

Ethan hesitated before making the drink, ever the seasoned bartender. He slammed it on the counter and pushed it toward her before taking a sip from his own glass, tension humming through him.

The woman picked up the tumbler and watched him with a carefully calculated expression as she slowly swirled the amber liquid, sending ice clinking against the glass.

"From the boorish way you just served me, I take it you know who I am?"

"Yes," Ethan said between gritted teeth. "You're Eveline Claude, the owner of *Le Secret*."

Eveline narrowed her blue eyes.

"I don't know which pisses me off more—the fact that you just made my name sound like a pit of snakes, or that you made *Le Secret* out to be a brothel in the worst slum in the world."

Ethan tilted his glass at her in a mocking toast. "I aim to please." He swallowed another mouthful of the fiery liquid and glared at Eveline. "Joe's not here, so whatever business you've got with him will have to wait."

"I'm not here for Joe."

Ethan's pulse jumped.

Eveline propped an elbow on the counter, lowered

her chin into the palm of her hand, and studied him curiously.

"I'm here to take a look at the man Joe risked his life to save."

Ethan inhaled sharply at her words, a fresh wave of agony washing over him. He would never forget the sight that had met his eyes when he'd come to in that alleyway and seen Joe.

The rage and remorse on Joe's face, as if he'd somehow failed Ethan. Joe's hand all swollen and bloodied where the skin had broken across his knuckles. The way Joe held Ethan against his broad chest while Ethan cried quietly, his body shaking in shock in the aftermath of the attack, his racing heart matching the wild beat he could hear under his cheek.

Joe hadn't touched him since that day. Not even once.

Eveline's eyes softened for the briefest moment before she narrowed them once more.

"You don't deserve him."

Her words were like a bucket of ice hitting Ethan head-on. He gasped, shock rendering him speechless. Anger surged through him in the next instant.

"Oh, yeah?" Ethan growled. "And what makes you think you're any better, bitch?"

Eveline blinked.

"Are you fucking kidding me, kid?" she said with a scowl.

Ethan crossed the gap to the counter and brought his face inches from Eveline's.

"So what?" he hissed. "You think just because Joe

seems to be under the mistaken impression that he still owes you for the past, you can dictate who is and isn't allowed in his life? That because you're a former escort with millions to your name, you can twist him around your little finger and make him do your bidding whenever you feel like it?"

Eveline's eyes flared, genuine surprise flashing across her face.

"He said that?" She glared at Ethan a second later. "And, hey, the rest of that was uncalled for! True, but uncalled for."

They glowered at each other for several seconds.

"I'm running dry," Eveline snapped, indicating her empty glass. "Pour me another one."

"Do it yourself," Ethan snarled.

Eveline grabbed him by the front of his shirt and tugged him toward her.

"Don't make me come over there and spank you, you shitty kid!" she spat.

"Shut up, you hag!" Ethan barked. "And, as far as money is concerned, I can make more than you with my eyes closed!"

Shit.

Ethan's face grew warm, angry with himself for letting a sliver of the truth slip.

"What?" Eveline barked.

She slipped her cell out of her purse, brought up a screen, and showed him some figures, her blue eyes shrinking to slits.

"You're saying you make more than this on your bartending salary, you snot-faced little prick?"

Ethan hesitated as he stared at the numbers on the cell phone.

Oh well. In for a penny, in for a pound. Besides, she's pissing me off big time.

He took his own phone out, tapped a password in, and brought up a screen of figures.

"Read it and weep, bitch." He shoved the phone in Eveline's face.

Eveline's eyes widened as she stared at the numbers, color draining from her beautiful face.

"Fuck. Me," she whispered hoarsely.

"No, thanks," Ethan said scathingly.

Eveline ignored him and squinted at his cell screen.

"Hey, you went for those shares? My guy told me they were a dud investment."

Ethan studied Eveline's phone closely. He sucked air between his teeth.

"Whoa, those are gonna crash in the next few weeks. You'd better shift them."

"Oh, yeah? Any suggestions?" Eveline pulled a pen out of her purse and slid a napkin toward him.

Ethan was halfway through writing details of a stocks and shares portfolio when he paused and stared blindly at the pen in his hand.

"What the fuck am I doing?"

Eveline chuckled. She leaned across the counter and dropped a gentle kiss on Ethan's cheek, startling him.

"You're helping out your new best friend," she said, a warm smile lighting up her face.

Ethan stared, stunned.

"What?"

Eveline sniffed.

"Don't make me say it again, you little shit."

Confusion washed through Ethan as he stared at the woman facing him. The animosity he had felt from Eveline had vanished and she sat gazing at him with an amiable if curious expression.

It was as if she'd been testing him.

"Why do you still call on him?" Ethan blurted out.

Eveline gave him a puzzled look.

"Joe," Ethan mumbled. "Why do you still call on him to work for you?"

Eveline watched him silently for a moment, her face softening.

"Has Joe ever told you about the gig he does for me on those occasions?"

Ethan shook his head, heat flooding his cheeks.

"No, but I can guess."

Eveline propped her chin in her hand again. "Well, you'd be guessing wrong, kiddo."

Ethan blinked. "What?"

Eveline played with her glass, her face melancholic.

"The client is a wealthy English widow whose son once visited *Le Secret*. Apparently, Joe is the spitting image of his father. He told his mother about it and she insisted on meeting Joe."

Ethan's heart drummed against his ribs at Eveline's words.

"You mean—"

Eveline smiled.

"It's never been about sex. They go for dinner once a month and just talk. She truly enjoys Joe's company and has never asked for more than that from him." Eveline sighed. "She and her husband were childhood sweethearts. They were married for over three decades before he died of a heart attack." Eveline paused, her eyes glinting. "Joe is such a softie, he would never refuse her."

Remorse twisted Ethan's stomach as he recalled the angry words he'd said to Joe that night at his apartment.

"Oh God, I've been such an idiot," he whispered.

"Eveline?" someone called out from across the club.

They turned and looked to where Joe stood watching them on the steps, surprise painted across his face.

"What are you doing here?" Joe said. His expression turned guarded as he headed toward the bar, his gaze swinging from Ethan to Eveline and back again.

Eveline flashed a bright smile at Joe. "I came to say hello to Ethan."

Joe slowed and arched an eyebrow, confusion darkening his eyes.

Eveline grinned.

"He and I are gonna be besties."

"Oh, yeah?" Ethan scoffed. "Since when?"

"Shut up, you shitty brat. Now, pour me that scotch."

CHAPTER TWELVE

JOE STARED AT THE DOOR BEFORE HIM, A BITTER TASTE IN his mouth. He grimaced when Ethan's face flashed in front of his eyes.

I can't believe I'm doing this. He'll kill me if he finds out.

Two hours had passed since Eveline had called him, alarm raising the pitch of her voice as she told him hastily of the escort who'd just bailed out on her and begged him for his help.

"I'm sorry about this, Joe," Eveline had blurted out. "You know I don't normally ask you to do this kind of stuff anymore, but I'm desperate here. This client has the power to crush my business and I've got no one else in my books who fits his demands." She'd hesitated for a couple of seconds. "Besides, he just wants to be dominated. There's no sex involved, so this will be a walk in the park for you."

Although Joe had seriously wanted to refuse her request, he owed Eveline too much to say no. It was only after he'd reluctantly agreed to bail her out that she'd sent him the details of the meetup. Joe's eyes had widened when he'd seen the name of the hotel.

It was the most expensive place in Tokyo, with the cheapest rooms costing upward from six hundred dollars a night. The key card he now held in his hand was for the two-grand-a-night penthouse suite, which he'd gained access to via a private elevator on the tenth floor.

Joe closed his eyes and dropped his forehead against the door's cool wooden surface.

She's a friend. Ethan will have to understand if he finds out. Besides, things aren't exactly going well for us right now.

It had been a month since Ethan's stalker had attacked and almost killed him.

The gut-wrenching remorse Joe had experienced on that day had still not faded, nor had his fear of what would have happened to Ethan had he not reached that alley at the time that he did. If anything, those bitter feelings only resurfaced afresh every time Joe looked at Ethan.

Joe knew he'd failed Ethan. Knew he'd failed to keep his promise to the young man who had slowly and insistently wormed his way inside his heart. Knew he'd failed to keep the person he cherished the most in this world safe.

Though Ethan had tried to talk to Joe on countless occasions since that day, his green eyes bereft of the accusation Joe felt he justly deserved, Joe had been unable to oblige him.

Joe didn't think he could stop himself from kissing

Ethan if they were on their own again. Joe knew he definitely wouldn't be able to stop himself from touching Ethan if that were to happen. And he was scared out of his mind at the thought of ever taking Ethan to bed.

Joe didn't want to hurt Ethan. Didn't want to break him. And he feared he would do just that if he gave in to the burning desire that now consumed him whenever they breathed the same air.

It took nearly losing Ethan for Joe to finally acknowledge just how much the cocky, green-eyed bartender had come to mean to him. How much he needed him. How much he craved not only Ethan's sinfully gorgeous body, but his beautiful heart and his bright soul.

Which made what he was about to do all that much harder to swallow.

Just get this shit over with and get a cab back to Saron. At least Ethan's not working tonight.

Joe frowned.

And Eveline owes me BIG time for this.

He straightened the cuff links of his blue Prada suit, steeled himself, and slipped the key card in the lock.

The suite was as stunning as he'd expected it to be, the glass wall spanning its length and width offering a staggering vista over the brightly lit city fifteen floors below.

Muted lighting softened the sleek lines of modern furniture dotting the dining area ahead, the amber beams sparkling off the well-stocked bar to his right. Joe strolled through and entered a large living space. A king-size bed dominated the sumptuous bedroom visible through the open doorway on the other side of the wooden floor. Joe caught a glimpse of a luxurious, glass walk-in shower and a hot tub overlooking Tokyo beyond it.

His gaze swung to the figure sitting on the couch to his left.

The man sat unmoving in a pool of shadows, his face and the lines of his body obscured, the background light from the city glancing off the tumbler in his hand.

God, I sure hope he doesn't want me to stick my dick in him 'cause I don't think I'll be able to get hard.

There was only one guy who'd had Joe's cock stiff and throbbing in the last year. And that guy was the one person he would never touch.

Joe allowed his lips to curve into a small smile, wishing it didn't come across as stiff as it felt. Eveline had told him the client wanted to remain anonymous.

"Hi there. I'm from *Le Se*—"

The man suddenly leaned forward. His glass clinked when he put it down heavily on the side table next to him. He bowed his head and dropped his face in his hands.

"Thank God," he whispered. "I thought you wouldn't come."

Joe froze. He knew that voice. Would have known it if he were blind.

"Ethan?" he said incredulously. He crossed the floor to a lamp and flicked the switch.

The shadows fled. The man sitting on the couch became visible.

"Ethan?!"

Ethan smiled tremulously and rose to his feet. He was dressed in a gunmetal-gray Louis Vuitton suit that hugged his body in all the right places, his crisp white shirt and green tie highlighting his stunning eyes.

"What the—" Joe stopped and scowled when he realized he'd been royally played.

He gritted his teeth, his emotions vacillating between shock and anger as he considered the man watching him from a few feet away. He froze when he suddenly registered the tremors running through Ethan's hands and body.

Joe's breath caught in his throat in the next instant. He blinked slowly, awareness striking him with the force of a speeding train and causing his heart to clench painfully.

He finally understood what this was.

What this beautiful man was trying to say to him.

This was Ethan surrendering himself to Joe, body and soul. Asking him not to be afraid. Telling him that he wanted this as badly as Joe did.

Begging him to take a chance on them.

Joe stared at Ethan for a timeless moment, his gaze searching the soulful green eyes that had filled his dreams for the last month. No, for the past year. He saw only love and hope there. And a sliver of nervousness that made his cock twitch.

Joe closed his eyes and groaned internally.

I give in.

The moment he thought those words, Joe sensed a huge weight drop off his shoulders. He opened his eyes and studied Ethan once more.

For the first time in weeks, Joe felt like he could breathe again. Felt like he could risk taking that chance he didn't dare take before.

Felt like he could finally touch this man like he'd been dying to do.

"Um, Joe?" Ethan said hesitantly, his fingers clenching by his sides.

Joe walked slowly over to the side table and lifted Ethan's glass to his mouth. He took a sip and savored the fine Scotch while he debated how much longer he would tease the young man before admitting the staggering conclusion he had just reached.

"Nice," Joe murmured. He licked his lips.

Ethan's gaze dropped to Joe's mouth, a moth to a flame. He swallowed hard, desire flashing in his emerald eyes.

"Look, I know you're angry right now," he started falteringly, "but this was the only—"

"Shut up, Mr. Client." Joe put the glass down and hooked a finger through the knot of Ethan's tie. He ignored his muttered protest and tugged him across the living space and through the open doorway into the bedroom at the far end. "Let's move to the main event, shall we?"

Joe grabbed Ethan's shoulder and shoved him gently toward the bed.

CHAPTER THIRTEEN

AIR WHOOSHED OUT OF ETHAN'S LUNGS AS HE LANDED ass-down on the edge of the mattress.

Oh, shit. He's fucking livid, isn't he?

He gulped and stared at the formidable man towering over him. His stomach dropped when he registered Joe's shuttered expression.

Ethan still couldn't believe he'd agreed to Eveline's cockamamie idea from when they'd met up for lunch five days ago.

"What?" Eveline had squealed, her blue eyes wide with shock. *"You two haven't had sex yet?!"*

Ethan had shushed her, his cheeks warming when her voice drew stares from across the chic restaurant where he was giving her advice on her stocks and shares portfolio over a free meal.

"I mean, what's the problem?" Eveline leaned across the table. "Are you impotent or something? I know Joe isn't, so—"

"I swear to God, every time you open your mouth, I

want to stab you with a fork," Ethan said between gritted teeth.

Eveline tut-tutted. "So, what is it then?"

Ethan found the words spilling out of him before he could stop himself. He told Eveline everything. About how he'd seen Joe for the first time a year ago and had fallen in love at first sight with the sexy club owner. About his plan to work at *Saron* to get closer to Joe and try and win his heart. About Joe finding out Ethan had a stalker and going into protective mode. About their date night and the one he'd spent in Joe's bed.

"He hasn't kissed me since that day. Hasn't touched me," Ethan said, his voice trembling slightly. "It's as if he doesn't even want to be in the same room as me anymore."

Eveline pursed her lips and watched him for a silent moment.

"I think what we have here is a serious case of Overly Protective Alpha Male Syndrome," she said finally. "Also known as The Guy Is So Crazy for You, He Daren't Touch You."

Ethan stared. "Come again?"

Eveline sighed and rolled her eyes.

"He loves you, you dumbass. Utterly and irrevocably. And he's probably going crazy right now stopping himself from touching you."

Ethan stared at her, his mouth opening and closing soundlessly. His pulse sped at Eveline's words. He didn't want to believe them yet wished so hard they were true he couldn't help but dig his nails into his palms.

"I—I don't understand!" he stammered.

Eveline reached across the table and took Ethan's hands. She uncurled his stiff fingers before gently holding them in her own.

"Joe thinks he failed you," she said quietly. "Failed to protect you. And it's killing him. He doesn't want to hurt you any more than you've been hurt already."

Ethan's stomach twisted at the look in Eveline's eyes.

"You mean, he thinks he'll—*hurt* me if we have sex?! Why would he—"

"Because he's afraid of losing control, you dope." Eveline sighed. "Joe has never truly been in love before." A sad smile curved her lips. "He thinks he has, but he hasn't, really. So he's scared. Scared of what he could do to you if he surrendered to his body's urge to, well—," she leaned in again and lowered her voice, "— fuck the living daylights out of your sweet little ass. And, FYI, there's a reason Joe was my best escort. He's a demon when it comes to stamina in the bedroom. And the guy's dick is a work of—"

The rest of Eveline's words were swallowed by Ethan's palm as he pressed a hand to her mouth, heat flooding his cheeks at the graphic image Eveline had just painted.

Eveline blinked rapidly.

"Oh my God, are you *blushing*?" She scrambled for her cell. "*So cute*! Let me take a picture and send it to Joe!"

"*Eveline!*" Ethan barked.

She'd spent the next hour coming up with the

ridiculous scenario now playing out before Ethan's eyes, even picking out a suit for him and telling him which hotel he should book for his meeting with Joe.

Ethan was wondering what he could say or do to soothe Joe's ire presently when the club owner spoke.

"*Soooo*," Joe pursed his lips and made the word drag out. "I've been told you like to be disciplined, Mr. Client."

Ethan froze, his train of thought completely derailed by Joe's words. He blinked at him owlishly.

"Huh?"

Joe ignored his dazed stare and strolled over to the nightstand. He opened the top drawer and studied its contents for a moment. Ethan blushed when Joe removed the box of condoms and the bottle of lube he'd put in there earlier, setting them on top.

"I see you came prepared," Joe murmured.

Confusion washed through Ethan when Joe suddenly dipped down on one knee and reached under the bed. A smile curved Joe's sculptured lips. He brought out a box, rose to his feet, and tipped it out on the mattress.

Ethan's heart stuttered when he saw the sinful black leather items scattering across the sheets. His eyes widened.

"And I gather you also like a bit of S&M," Joe continued silkily.

He picked up a leather riding crop and flicked it gently against his palm.

Ethan's belly clenched at the sight of Joe with the

whip, not sure whether it was unease or excitement that had his pulse hammering away in his veins.

"Look, I have no fucking idea how those got there," he said stiffly. "I sure as hell didn't—" Ethan paused, realization striking him like a bolt of lightning. He scowled with his next breath. "Oh, that *witch*! I'm *SO* gonna screw up her portfo—" Ethan bit the inside of his cheek and swallowed the rest of his words when he saw the puzzled light that flashed in Joe's eyes.

"Is there something you want to tell me, Ethan?" Joe snapped the whip against his palm again and walked slowly around the bed.

Ethan's stomach flipped-flopped at Joe's predatory stance.

"Um, nope, I'm good," he mumbled shakily.

"You sure?" Joe said softly.

He stopped in front of Ethan, nudged Ethan's knees open with one powerful leg, and stepped inside the cradle of Ethan's thighs. Ethan gasped when Joe tilted his chin up with the end of the whip. He gulped at the cool feel of the leather against his skin and the heat of Joe's body so close to him, his heart pounding so hard he thought he would have a heart attack.

"Looks like someone needs to be punished," Joe said gruffly.

He reached out, curled his fingers in Ethan's hair, and tugged Ethan's head back as he trailed the whip down Ethan's throat.

Oh God.

Ethan swallowed a whimper and squeezed his eyes

shut, mortified at the thrill that accompanied the dread rising inside him.

"Just do it!" he said.

Joe's fingers stilled on him.

"Do what?"

"You want to hit me, right?" Ethan bit his lower lip and kept his eyes closed, not wanting to see the anger and disappointment on Joe's face. "Go ahead. Do it."

Silence filled the space between them, so heavy and tense Ethan felt a whisper would shatter it.

"Shit," Joe said huskily.

Ethan blinked his eyes open and looked up at him. His breath caught in his throat when Joe dropped the whip and knelt on the floor before him.

Joe raised his hands and cradled Ethan's face as if he were the most precious thing in the whole world, his hazel eyes glittering with emotion.

"I was only joking, you fool," he said with a tremulous chuckle, his fingers trembling on Ethan's skin. "And I know Eveline never intended for me to use those on you." He indicated the bondage materials on the bed. "She was only teasing you."

Joe dropped the softest kiss on Ethan's forehead and took him in his arms, hugging him gently to his broad chest.

"I would never do anything to hurt you," he whispered in Ethan's hair. "Ever."

Hotness flooded Ethan's chest. His vision blurred. He wrapped his arms around Joe and held on for dear life, not quite believing that this was happening. That

Joe was saying these words to him. Words Ethan had been dying to hear for as long as he'd known him.

They stayed like that for a long time, their hearts thundering against each other's, unspoken words whirling around them. The air gradually thickened, so taut with raw need and sexual tension that Ethan's breath hitched in his throat. Joe's scent and heat were overwhelming his senses and threatening to make him lose his mind.

Joe pulled back and tipped Ethan's chin with his finger, his feverish expression telling Ethan he was also close to losing it.

"Tell me, Ethan. What do you want me to do?"

The sexy smile that curved Joe's lips made Ethan's pulse flutter wildly.

"Tell me your dirtiest fantasies. Everything you've ever wanted me to do to you." Joe leaned in and brought his lips to Ethan's right ear, his stubble tickling his skin. "I will do it all." He whirled his tongue against the shell before sucking and gently biting down on the sensitive lobe.

Oh, sweet Jesus!

CHAPTER FOURTEEN

Joe bit back a curse when Ethan shuddered under his hands, back arching like a cat. He wasn't sure how much longer he could hold on to his self-control. Not when Ethan was responding so hotly and sweetly to his touch.

Ethan swallowed and stared dazedly at Joe when he sat back on his heels.

"Tell me, Ethan," Joe ordered thickly.

He raised a hand to Ethan's mouth and stroked his lower lip roughly with his thumb.

"I—" Ethan swallowed, his hot breath washing across the sensitive pad of Joe's finger, sending heat straight to Joe's cock. "I want you to—"

"Yes?" Joe coaxed. "You want me to do what, Ethan?"

Ethan shivered, color painting his cheekbones a dull red.

"I want you to strip me."

Joe stifled a groan at the shyly whispered words.

He lowered his hand to Ethan's silk tie and undid the knot slickly before gliding it from around his neck and dropping it on the floor. Joe reached for the buttons of Ethan's shirt next and unfastened them one by one.

Ethan trembled when Joe pulled the lower ends of the fabric out from his pants. Joe parted the material before pushing the shirt off Ethan's shoulders and down his arms, taking the suit jacket with it.

Joe paused and stared at the delicious expanse of toned muscles and honey-colored skin exposed before his greedy eyes. His mouth went dry when his gaze skimmed Ethan's six-pack and followed the thin trail of dark blond hair arrowing down from his navel and disappearing behind his buckle.

So goddamn sexy.

Ethan twitched when Joe grazed his chest with his fingers. Joe trailed his hand down slowly, his own arousal thickening painfully at the way Ethan shivered and jerked beneath his touch, rib cage rising and falling erratically with his breathing.

Joe paused deliberately when he reached Ethan's belt, as much to tease the bartender as to give himself a moment to cool his raging libido.

"Then what, Ethan?"

Joe hooked a finger through the leather and started unbuckling Ethan, the sounds loud and wickedly dirty in the charged stillness. He tugged the belt out of Ethan's pants and dropped it on the floor, the metal clinking loudly against the wood.

"Tell me what you want me to do after that, Ethan."

Joe went still, his fingers on Ethan's zipper. Watching. Waiting.

Ethan's lips parted, his breaths coming in labored pants, his green eyes dilated with desire, his erection straining a hairbreadth from Joe's touch.

"I want you to kiss me," he moaned.

Joe moved. He brought his mouth down on Ethan's and took his eager lips in a torrid kiss that had Ethan flexing his hips off the bed and Joe cursing silently.

"Where else do you want me to kiss you?" Joe grated out a moment later, pleasure sending his own cock pulsing and throbbing against the zipper of his pants.

He dipped his head and nipped at Ethan's throat, loving how Ethan tensed and shivered all over again.

"Oh God!" Ethan gasped. "*Everywhere!*"

"Everywhere?" Joe kissed and laved the sensitive skin he'd bitten with his tongue, his heart slamming against his ribs.

He danced a finger along the hard length of Ethan's cock and almost groaned when the young man lifted off the bed again, a throaty cry leaving his lips as he flexed his hips against Joe's hand.

"Even here?" Joe teased.

"*Yes!*"

It took but seconds to free Ethan's swollen member. Joe palmed the flushed, glistening shaft and took it in his mouth, the groan finally leaving his throat as he swirled his tongue around the head and tasted the sweet, salty fluid pearling at the tip.

𝄞

OH. MY. GOD.

Ethan couldn't stop the incoherent cries and moans ripping from his throat as Joe licked and sucked him, his powerful mouth and jaw sending jolts of pure pleasure shooting through Ethan while he swallowed him deep, his thick tongue repeatedly flicking the sensitive head of Ethan's cock, his stubbled chin grazing Ethan's balls.

Ethan fell back on the bed, hands rising to cover his face. He bit down on his fists to muffle the wickedly wanton noises he was making, shocked at how loud he was being. He shuddered when Joe suddenly released his cock, the wet popping sound making his ass twitch. Ethan blinked and looked down dazedly.

Joe reached up and pulled Ethan's hands from his mouth.

"Don't," he said hoarsely, hazel eyes dark with passion. "You're so fucking sexy, Ethan. I love it when you cry and moan. Please, let me hear you."

Ethan let out a low groan as he watched the man kneeling between his legs take him in his mouth again. Joe's eyes fluttered closed as he concentrated on pleasing Ethan, his fingers stroking and squeezing the tightening sac below Ethan's shaft.

Ethan fell back on the bed and gave in to Joe. His climax washed over him too soon, his body overwhelmed by the touch and feel of the man he'd wanted for so long. His belly tensed and trembled as he arched off the bed, hips thrusting into the hot mouth swallowing his cock and cum, sobs wrenched from his lips at the incredible pleasure Joe was giving him.

Ethan fell back on the sheets after a timeless moment of ecstasy, his entire body drenched with sweat, his breaths coming hard and fast, his ass pulsing at the fading waves of his intense orgasm.

"What next, Ethan?" Joe said thickly. "What do you want me to do next?"

JOE'S DICK STRAINED PAINFULLY AGAINST HIS PANTS AS HE stared at Ethan.

He was right. Watching Ethan climax was the most wicked, sensual, filthy thing he'd ever witnessed, the sight as addictive as the finest drug.

Joe stripped Ethan of the rest of his clothes while the latter still shuddered from his powerful orgasm. His cock throbbed when he exposed the sweet mole on Ethan's right hip and glimpsed the shadowy cleft beneath his balls. Joe dipped his chin, unable to resist the urge to kiss the sexy birthmark. A smile curved his lips when Ethan whimpered and trembled.

"Tell me, Ethan," Joe commanded again in a sultry voice, his gaze skimming up the golden body beneath his mouth and meeting a pair of glazed green eyes.

"I want you—" Ethan gasped and let out a little hum of pleasure when Joe nipped at his skin again. "I want you to *fuck* me!"

Joe's cock pulsed at Ethan's words. He rose and stripped rapidly, his breathing ragged as he shrugged out of his suit and stepped out of his briefs. Ethan's eyes widened when he took in Joe's impressive erection. He scooted up the bed, making space for Joe as the latter climbed onto the mattress with his aching cock at full mast.

Joe cursed when Ethan reached out with trembling fingers and touched his throbbing shaft.

"Can I?" Ethan whispered, his eyes shyly rising to meet Joe's.

Joe nodded, not trusting himself to speak.

He swallowed a groan when Ethan went on all fours before him and gently licked him. Air hissed out of Joe in the next instant when Ethan wrapped his clever tongue and lips around him, taking him deep inside his mouth, sucking sweetly.

"Fuck."

Joe dropped his hands to Ethan's head, fingers twisting gently in the thick blond curls. His hips soon started a rhythmic roll that sent his cock gliding wetly in and out of Ethan's mouth, spasms of pleasure shooting through him with each strong contraction of the sexy jaw clamped tightly around him and the sinful flicks of Ethan's tongue against his sensitive shaft.

Too soon, Joe's orgasm wound down his spine, gathering at the base, tickling his tightening balls, clenching his belly. He groaned and tugged at Ethan's head a moment later, trying to get him off his cock as he felt the first wave of his climax rise through him.

Ethan resisted, hands rising to grip Joe's hips, jaw opening wider to take him to the hilt. Joe cursed when he felt the head of his dick hit the hot depths of Ethan's throat. Ethan grunted and sucked deeply once, then twice.

Joe exploded on Ethan's tongue, his cock pulsing inside the hungry mouth greedily devouring him, his breaths leaving his nose in harsh pants as he clenched his teeth and closed his eyes, his head falling back with the potent pleasure of his orgasm.

CHAPTER FIFTEEN

ETHAN MOANED AS JOE THRUST HIS THICK, PULSATING shaft inside his mouth, his own ass and dick twitching in response to the awe-inspiring view of the man he loved climaxing above him. He swallowed the thick, salty liquid flooding his throat, the taste and smell of Joe's intoxicating scent on his tongue so arousing he felt his own cock throb and leak pre-cum.

Joe gently tugged him off, teeth biting into his lower lip when Ethan milked his glistening dick with his tongue until the very last second before he reluctantly let go. He pushed Ethan down to the bed and covered him with his body, his powerful frame sinking them both into the mattress.

"Give me a minute," Joe rasped, his chest heaving from his climax.

Ethan nodded against his shoulder, his entire body tingling where Joe's bare skin kissed his, loving the feel of Joe's weight on him.

"It's okay, old man." Ethan patted Joe's back lightly

and grinned when Joe's body shook with laughter against his.

"You brat," Joe said, chuckling. "Just you wait. I'm gonna fuck you so thoroughly, you're not gonna be able to walk out of here tomorrow."

Ethan's ass quivered and his cock flexed at the passionate threat.

"Sure, old man," he said hoarsely.

Joe propped himself on his elbows a moment later and kissed Ethan hard.

"Okay, let's properly start round one now, shall we?" he murmured against Ethan's lips.

Ethan blinked.

"We just had round one. And two."

Joe tut-tutted and shook his head, hazel eyes glinting with laughter while his face projected mock disappointment.

"Blow jobs don't count as rounds. Besides, that was just a bit of light relief."

"*Light—light relief?*" Ethan spluttered. "I've never moaned so loud in my life!"

Joe arched an eyebrow. "Really?"

Ethan shivered when Joe dipped his head and kissed his throat before bringing his lips to his left ear.

"I can't wait to hear what kind of sounds you're gonna make when I'm deep inside you."

Oh God.

JOE CHUCKLED WHEN ETHAN MOANED BREATHILY AND flexed his hips, his swelling cock pushing against Joe's belly. Joe kissed Ethan again. A shudder raced through him when he invaded the hot, dark space of Ethan's mouth and tasted himself on Ethan's tongue.

By the time he released Ethan's lips, Joe's own cock ached and throbbed against Ethan's hip. Though he wanted nothing more than to part Ethan's legs and explore the shadowy cleft he'd glimpsed before, it was far too soon for that. Not when there was so much sexy real estate to explore.

He moved his mouth to Ethan's ear, gently biting it before nudging Ethan's chin up with his head and exploring his delectable throat.

Ethan arched to give him better access, his pulse fluttering wildly against Joe's lips, his fingers digging into Joe's shoulders as he shivered and twitched. Ethan opened his legs, his knees rising slightly before dropping to the sides, unconsciously inviting Joe into the cradle of his body.

Joe swallowed a groan when their groins kissed intimately; he wondered how the hell he was going to last when the man below him was surrendering himself so sweetly to him.

He shifted his hands to Ethan's chest, stroking his hot skin and firm muscles before lightly grazing them with his nails, his lips and tongue following the path of his fingers.

Ethan cursed when Joe rubbed his thumbs across his nipples.

"Like that?" Joe murmured.

"*Yes!*" Ethan hissed.

Joe pinched and twisted the hard, brown nubs before taking them in his mouth, greedily sucking and laving them. Ethan went wild beneath him, his engorged cock leaving a wet trail of pre-cum against Joe's belly while he whimpered and moaned.

Joe grunted at the potent scent of Ethan's arousal, his own dick doing push-ups against the mattress between Ethan's thighs. He moved south, kissing and nipping at the quivering muscles of Ethan's toned belly.

Joe's mouth finally found the mole on Ethan's right hip. He laved and sucked at the birthmark, his hands gripping Ethan's waist tightly when the latter writhed helplessly against the sheets.

"You—you really like that spot, don't you?" Ethan gasped.

"Uh-huh," Joe murmured against his honey skin.

A shudder ran through Ethan.

"I—I've got another one."

Joe raised his head, ears perking. He swallowed a groan at the wickedly sexy sight of an aroused Ethan.

Ethan covered his face with his hands, ears flaming.

Joe's cock throbbed at Ethan's obvious embarrassment. His instincts told him he was going to love where that other mole was.

"Tell me where it is, Ethan," Joe purred, moving his head to flick the tip of Ethan's trembling cock with his tongue.

"*Oh!*" Ethan arched off the mattress.

Joe repeated the move.

"*Oh God!*" Ethan gasped, his cock jerking against Joe's lips. "Down there! It's down there!"

Joe stared at him.

Holy fuck.

He moved, his heart slamming against his ribs as he parted Ethan's thighs and lifted them in the air.

A shudder ran through Joe when he finally saw the pink pucker of tight folds guarding Ethan's entrance. The mole sat directly in the middle of the stretch of tight skin running down to Ethan's ass from his balls.

Joe rose, grabbed a pillow and the lube, and settled back down between Ethan's thighs.

Ethan fisted his hands in the sheets when Joe nudged the pillow under his butt. Joe stared at Ethan up the length of his body and saw his lips part in anticipation of what was to come, his passion-glazed eyes locking on Joe's. The expression in the green depths was so full of raw need Joe knew it wouldn't be long before he sank his cock inside Ethan's body and gave them both what they so very much wanted.

Joe flashed Ethan a filthy grin, placed his hands against the back of Ethan's thighs, and pushed them up.

ETHAN'S BREATH STILLED AT THE DIRTY, SEXY SMILE JOE gave him from where he lay between his legs.

Joe's eyes grew heavy-lidded when he took hold of Ethan's thighs and lifted them. He dipped his head, his lower face disappearing past Ethan's crotch until only his eyes showed, hot hazel gaze still locked on Ethan's.

Ethan curled his fingers tighter into the bedsheets when Joe's breath washed across the deliciously sensitive skin below his balls.

Fire shot through him at the first flick of Joe's tongue.

"*Oh!*"

Ethan's toes twitched and curled midair, his spine arching off the mattress.

Joe flicked his tongue against his mole again and again before really going to town on him with his whole mouth.

Ethan threw his head back into the pillow, eyes staring blindly at the ceiling for a moment before he squeezed them shut, pleasure jolting him with every kiss and suck of Joe's wicked lips.

"*Joe!*"

Ethan chanted Joe's name over and over again. He let go of the sheets and gripped the dark head between his thighs, his fingers twisting in the thick locks as tension started spiraling down his spine.

"*Please!*"

Joe's mouth stilled on Ethan at his sudden plea.

"Please what, Ethan?" he growled, his voice heavy with passion. "Tell me."

Ethan groaned, embarrassment bringing a flood of heat to his cheeks. He flexed his hips, silently telling Joe where he wanted his mouth next.

"Say it, Ethan."

Ethan shuddered at Joe's commanding tone.

"I want your mouth on me!" he moaned. "Down there!"

Joe moved, his teeth nibbling at a sensitive spot on Ethan's right thigh.

"You mean, you want me to kiss your hole?"

Joe's crude words had Ethan's hips rising off the pillow once more, his climax building at the base of his balls and spine.

"Yes!" Ethan breathed.

"Want me to lick it?"

Ethan's cock throbbed painfully.

"Oh God, yes!"

"Do you want my tongue inside you, Ethan?"

CHAPTER SIXTEEN

The wild sound Ethan made at Joe's last taunting words drew a groan of need from Joe's own throat.

Joe dipped his head and gave Ethan what they both so desperately wanted, flicking his tongue across the twitching hole begging for his attention. Joe's cock pulsed against the bed, his senses drowning in Ethan's intoxicating scent while he tasted his sinfully sexy opening, Ethan's sultry cries and moans inflaming him further.

Joe closed his lips around the quivering pucker and sucked before probing Ethan's entrance with his tongue. His fingers bit into Ethan's thighs while he maintained his hot assault, holding Ethan in place while the latter bucked and writhed in pleasure.

Ethan's folds trembled and contracted before finally unfurling.

Joe grunted and dipped his tongue inside, licking the sensitive nerves along the rim.

"*Joe!*" Ethan shouted. "*Oh God!*"

Ethan's spine lifted off the mattress, his climax sending his cock pulsing jets of cum over his quivering belly.

The way Ethan arched his neck, muscles cording while his hands fisted into the pillow beneath his head, his unfocused eyes wide as he stared blindly at the ceiling, his mouth open on incoherent cries, his hips rolling uncontrollably as his orgasm tore through him—all of it was too much for Joe.

He cursed, grabbed a condom from the box on the nightstand, and rose up onto his knees. He gritted his teeth as he sheathed and lubed his painfully stiff cock.

Ethan shuddered and blinked beneath him. His gaze locked on Joe's hard shaft. He bit his lower lip and bent his legs, hands reaching down to grab the backs of his knees, thighs falling on the pillow beneath his butt as he opened himself for Joe.

Joe groaned at the wickedly sinful sight. He had never seen anything as beautiful as Ethan surrendering himself to him, green eyes full of desire and trust. He held Ethan's right thigh and brought his lubed fingers to Ethan's hole.

Ethan gasped as Joe probed him, rubbing and playing with the slick folds until they opened for him once more. He moaned when Joe slipped one finger and then a second inside, stretching him before slowly thrusting in and out.

Joe licked his lips as he watched his slick fingers get swallowed by Ethan's body, gently exploring and searching with each delicious slide. Anticipation brought a surge of heat to his cock at the thought of being buried deep inside that place.

"*Oh!*"

Joe paused and watched Ethan's eyes widen, pupils dilating with pleasure. He stroked Ethan's sweet spot again and was rewarded with a throaty gasp and the hole he was invading clamping down around him tightly, drawing a hiss of pleasure from his own lips.

Joe continued his exquisite torture, driving his fingers in and out of the spasming hot passage, not stopping until Ethan climaxed violently beneath him, sweat beading his face and body as he repeatedly cried out Joe's name.

Only then did he pull his fingers out and guide his aching cock to Ethan's hole. Joe grabbed the backs of Ethan's calves and brought his legs up, dropping Ethan's ankles on his shoulders.

Ethan whimpered, color painting red flags on his cheekbones as he looked up at Joe between his spread legs, his expression an intoxicating mix of passion and vulnerability.

Joe moved up and braced his hands on either side of Ethan's head, pushing Ethan's legs toward his chest. Joe stared down at Ethan heatedly, cock pulsing against Ethan's wet opening.

"You're so fucking gorgeous," Joe growled. "I want to lock you up. Somewhere no other man can look at you or touch you. You're too damn sexy for your own good, Ethan Skye."

Ethan stilled then. He stared at Joe for a moment before his lips curved in a tremulous smile.

"There's one way you can make sure no one else comes after me, Joe."

Joe's breath caught in his throat at the crystal-clear emotion displayed on Ethan's face.

"All you have to do is claim me," Ethan whispered, his eyes glinting with a wet sheen.

Joe froze. Then, he bowed his back and pressed his forehead against Ethan's. He could no longer deny his feelings for the man beneath him.

He was utterly, irrevocably, stupidly in love with Ethan Skye.

"Then, I claim you," Joe whispered. "From now on and forever."

He dropped a searing kiss on Ethan's mouth and kept his gaze locked on the glazed green eyes beneath him as he slowly flexed his hips.

They both groaned as Joe's cock pushed against Ethan's entrance, parting it, entering the tight passage beyond.

&a.

ETHAN GASPED AT THE INCREDIBLE SENSATION OF JOE penetrating him, his mind and heart still reeling from Joe's husky admission a second ago. He was so deliriously happy, he would have shouted it from the rooftops had his voice not been so hoarse from all the delicious cries and moans the man had wrenched from him.

Despite Joe's size, there was not as much burn and sting as Ethan had expected, but rather the most amazing feeling of fullness and the exquisite heat of Joe's body inside him. Ethan blinked, unable to look away from the passion-filled hazel eyes above him, Joe's dilated pupils telling him how good it felt to him too as he continued pushing and gliding inside, not stopping until all of him was in to the hilt.

Joe paused for a moment and closed his eyes, sweat beading his upper lip and forehead.

"Fuck!" he gasped. "You have no idea what it feels like to be inside you, Ethan."

Ethan moaned and dug his heels into Joe's shoulders, his hole clenching around the rock-hard shaft impaling his body.

"Show me," he breathed.

Joe cursed and rolled his hips, bringing his cock out of Ethan's slick opening before sliding back home.

Brightness exploded behind Ethan's eyes as the head of Joe's shaft found his prostate.

Joe set a steady, punishing pace, his hips flexing slow and deep, each thrust eliciting such intense pleasure that Ethan could only cry out incoherently.

JOE CLENCHED HIS JAW AND STARED AT ETHAN AS THE latter writhed and arched beneath him, ass lifting off the pillow to meet Joe's every thrust, heels biting demandingly into Joe's shoulders, urging him on. Joe fisted his hands in the sheets on either side of Ethan's head and dropped his gaze to where his cock plunged in and out of Ethan's hole, the sight so arousing he almost came there and then.

Joe could feel his orgasm gathering at the base of his spine, the spiraling sweet tension winding deliciously through him with each delectable constriction of Ethan's passage. He gritted his teeth, willing himself to curb the roll of his hips, not wanting to lose control, afraid he would hurt Ethan if he drove into him as wildly as he so very much wanted to.

Ethan suddenly stiffened, Joe's name leaving his lips with a guttural sound that came from deep inside his chest, his eyes widening before glazing over, his cock pulsing fiercely as he climaxed.

Joe's balls tightened as Ethan's hole clamped and spasmed around his dick, sucking him in and holding on tightly while he continued to convulse beneath him. The noises Ethan was making were so insanely sexy, Joe knew he would never forget them for as long as he lived.

Joe's own climax rushed through him in the next instant, blinding waves that seared his mind with white light. Harsh grunts left his throat as he pumped his pulsing cock erratically in and out of Ethan.

Ethan curled his hands around Joe's forearms where they were braced on either side of his head. His fingers bit into Joe's flesh as he lifted his head off the pillow, seeking Joe's kiss.

Joe obliged, dipping his head and meeting Ethan's lips, invading his mouth while the aftershocks of their orgasms continued to course deliciously through them.

Their tongues twisted in a dance that mimicked their mating, their breaths blowing out through their noses in harsh, fast pants.

CHAPTER SEVENTEEN

ETHAN'S HEART RACED WILDLY, HIS ENTIRE BODY trembling with fading pulses of ecstasy. Joe lowered Ethan's ankles from his shoulders and wrapped them around his waist before collapsing against him, his throbbing cock still wedged deep inside Ethan's body.

They lay like that for a while, their ragged breathing loud above the blood roaring in Ethan's ears. The feel of Joe's heart pounding against Ethan's chest was so sweet he almost cried.

He had never known this. This bliss.

More than the potent pleasure he knew he would find in Joe's arms, more than the mind-blowing orgasms the man he loved had delivered with his hands, mouth, and body, Ethan cherished the incredible happiness swirling around and through him.

Joe finally lifted his head off the pillow and looked down at Ethan.

"Ready for round two?" he said huskily.

Ethan widened his eyes and blushed when he felt

Joe swelling inside him. He bit his lip and nodded. A moan left his throat as Joe slipped out of his body.

Ethan watched Joe discard the used condom and grab a fresh one.

He reached out and stayed Joe's hands as he started ripping the foil, his body moving before his mind could fully process his sudden yearning.

"No."

Joe blinked at him.

Ethan swallowed, stunned at the hot, dirty wish he'd just expressed with that single word, wondering if he'd shocked Joe.

He had never taken a man bare before. Never experienced someone's naked cock filling his hole. Never known what it felt like to have his insides filled with his lover's cum.

Ethan glanced at Joe's glistening, rock-hard dick. He swallowed a moan of need, his ass twitching. He wanted it inside him so bad, he could taste it.

Joe's eyes darkened.

"You sure?" he said, his voice heavy with desire.

Ethan nodded, his cheeks flaming.

Joe placed the condom on the nightstand and settled back down between Ethan's thighs.

"Just so you know," he said, dropping a hot kiss on his chest, "I'm clean."

Ethan swallowed. "So am I."

He sat up and looped his arms around Joe's neck.

Joe drew himself onto his knees and hugged him back, their stiff cocks pressing against each other's belly, eliciting a groan from both of them.

"Joe?" Ethan whispered.

"Yeah?" Joe murmured, running his hands down Ethan's spine to his butt, parting his cheeks.

Ethan sucked air between his teeth as Joe poured some lube onto his hands and probed Ethan's opening with his slick fingers, sliding two in, stretching him, rubbing the sensitive rim.

"I want to see it," Ethan moaned as tingles shot through his cock from his ass.

"See what?" Joe said, his fingers busy working Ethan's hole, driving him crazy.

Ethan brought his mouth to Joe's right ear and bit the lobe.

"I want to see you lose control."

Joe went still against him. He drew back slightly, lines marring his brow.

Ethan cradled Joe's face and pressed his lips to Joe's mouth before the latter could utter a protest, pouring everything he had into the kiss.

Joe groaned, his hips rolling hard against Ethan's.

"I don't want to hurt you," he said thickly.

"You won't." Ethan dropped his forehead against Joe's. "Please, Joe. I'm begging you," he breathed.

❦

FUCK.

Joe felt his self-restraint finally snap at Ethan's sexy plea, the sound so loud in his head he wondered if Ethan heard it. He moved, swooping to take Ethan's mouth in a soul-searing kiss, his fingers biting into Ethan's butt cheeks.

Ethan gasped, the throaty sound swallowed by Joe's hungry lips.

Joe hooked his hands under Ethan's thighs and lifted him up against his body before backing him toward the wall. He pulled a pair of pillows under Ethan's ass and behind his lower back before settling his spine against the headboard.

"Wrap your arms and legs around me," Joe ordered.

Ethan obeyed his gruff command, hooking his arms around Joe's shoulders and locking his strong thighs around Joe's waist. His crossed heels came to rest on Joe's butt cheeks, his cock trembling as it kissed Joe's belly, his twitching hole perfectly positioned against the tip of Joe's aching dick.

The flush of color on Ethan's cheeks and the thrill darkening his green eyes told Joe all he needed to know about what he was feeling in that moment.

Joe flexed his hips and penetrated Ethan in one smooth thrust, gliding in all the way to the hilt, fire licking his shaft and balls at the incredible feel of entering the man he loved bareback.

Ethan cried out and dropped his head back against the headboard, body arching deliciously against him, his cock leaking hot pre-cum on Joe's skin.

Joe braced his hands on the wall above the bed and kissed Ethan's exposed throat.

"Get ready," he said huskily.

IT WAS ALL THE WARNING ETHAN GOT BEFORE JOE thrust up powerfully, lifting Ethan's entire body up against the headboard in a sensuous roll.

"*Oh!*"

Pleasure speared through Ethan, so blinding it sent red spots flashing across his vision.

Joe flexed his hips again, pulling his cock out of Ethan's pulsing wet passage before driving back in to the hilt with a harsh grunt.

"*Oh God!*"

Ethan's orgasm hit him with the force of a freight train. He shouted Joe's name over and over again as he shuddered and convulsed, his nails scoring Joe's back, his heels digging into Joe's flesh.

Joe took Ethan's mouth in a blistering kiss, swallowing his cries while he maintained his sweetly savage pace, his hips rolling deep and hard, taking Ethan like he wanted to, driving him close to the edge once more.

"You okay?" Joe gasped, face slick with sweat and cheeks flushed as he stared hotly at Ethan.

Ethan bit his lower lip so hard he almost drew blood.

"*More! I want more!*" he cried.

§

*J*ESUS, HOW CAN HE BE SO—

Joe groaned when Ethan's hole clamped tightly around his rigid shaft. A tortured sob left Ethan's throat as he came apart again, his hot passage pulsing violently with his climax.

Joe fisted one hand against the wall and dropped the other to Ethan's butt, holding him in place while he took him. He lowered his face against Ethan's neck and pressed his lips to Ethan's skin, tasting his sweat and reveling in the flutter of his racing pulse.

Joe closed his eyes and lost himself in Ethan, plunging deep and wild into him, surrendering himself completely to his body's carnal instincts, savoring the sweet bliss his soul derived from mating with the one his heart had chosen.

The first wave of his orgasm hit him moments later, the pleasure so intense it was almost pain.

Ethan blinked dazedly at him, green eyes full of wonder and love as Joe grunted and came inside him, throbbing cock pulsing out streams of hot cum, flooding Ethan's insides with his seed. Ethan's lashes fluttered closed in the next moment, mouth opening on a shout as he climaxed again, his gorgeous face twisting with delicious rapture.

Joe took Ethan's lips in a hard kiss, his breaths huffing loudly out of his nose as he continued driving his still-hard cock inside Ethan's throbbing hole, bringing him to one toe-curling dry orgasm after another.

It wasn't until Joe had climaxed for the third time that he finally sagged on the bed, his thighs trembling, sweat dripping from his face and rolling down Ethan's chest. He closed his arms around Ethan and fell back onto the mattress.

Ethan landed limply on top of him, body still shivering and twitching from his multiple climaxes, his breathing labored and his heart racing against Joe's chest.

Joe lifted a hand and stroked away a sweat-slicked, blond lock from Ethan's forehead before kissing his hot skin.

"You okay?"

Ethan slowly lifted his head, cheeks flushed and eyes sultry with pleasure. He nodded weakly and dropped his head against Joe's chest, too breathless to speak.

"I take back that old-man statement," he managed a moment later.

Joe chuckled. He swallowed a groan in the next instant as Ethan's hole spasmed on his cock where he was still buried deep inside him. He withdrew slowly, grimacing when Ethan tightened instinctively around him.

Ethan moaned when Joe slipped out completely. A soft cry left his lips a second later.

"Oh!" He looked up at Joe, ears flaming.

Joe grinned, fingers finding the warm cum oozing out of Ethan's body. He slapped Ethan's butt slightly.

"We need to clean you up, sweet cheeks."

Joe sat up and dragged Ethan off the bed and toward the bathroom.

A moan halted his steps. Joe looked around and groaned at the sight that met his eyes, his dick twitching to life once more.

Jesus, he's fucking killing me.

Ethan bit his lip, pleasure darkening his eyes as he stared at the sticky white trail running down the inside of his left thigh, his cock swelling with fresh arousal.

"So, where do you want to do this? The shower or the hot tub?" Joe said hoarsely.

Ethan's gaze dropped to Joe's hardening shaft. "Joe," he breathed in a voice full of need.

Joe swallowed.

"Both it is then."

He tugged Ethan inside the luxurious bathroom.

CHAPTER EIGHTEEN

"Wow," Eveline muttered. "You look like the cat that not only got the cream, but also inherited the deeds to the cream factory." She grinned salaciously.

Joe narrowed his eyes at her across the table.

"I still haven't forgiven you for that stunt you pulled."

Over a week had passed since Joe and Ethan finally consummated their relationship during one spectacular night of mind-blowing sex. It was Sunday evening and they'd invited Eveline, Cam, and Gabe over for takeout and drinks.

"Really?" Eveline's gaze shifted to where Ethan sat next to Joe. She arched an eyebrow. "Even though the guy beside you looks like a blushing virgin who's had his flower plucked for the first time?"

Ethan shoved a prawn in his mouth, ears flaming.

"Oh." Eveline blinked. "I'm sorry. Should I have said *deflowered* instead?"

"Sweet Jesus," Ethan groaned. "Shut the fuck up, Evie!"

Joe's lips twitched at the nickname. The fact that Ethan and Eveline got on like a house on fire was something he could never have anticipated in a million years. It was like watching a panther become besties with a lioness.

"Still not good enough?" Eveline said with a pout. "How about roast the broomstick? Butter the biscuit? Dip the crane in the oil well? Had a hot beef injec—"

Ethan jerked Joe by the front of his T-shirt while Eveline listed more euphemisms.

"You brought her to the party," he growled. "Now, fucking deal with it!"

Joe swallowed the laughter bubbling inside him and maintained a deadpan expression. "This is your punishment for tricking me."

"What are you guys talking about?" Gabe said from across the way.

They all stared at him. Gabe reached for his glass, his expression still puzzled.

Eveline narrowed her eyes at Cam.

"Jesus, Sorvino, how the hell did you end up with such a sweetie?" Eveline leaned toward Gabe, a sexy, filthy smile curving her lips. "Fuck-ing, darling" she enunciated. "We're talking about Joe and Ethan finally making whoopee."

Gabe choked on his drink and dissolved in a fit of coughs.

Cam thumped him on the back and scowled at Eveline.

"Will you stop trying to kill my boyfriend?" His expression softened as he looked at Joe and Ethan. He flashed them a grin. "Congrats, you two."

Eveline's jaw dropped.

"My God," she muttered. "I never thought I'd see the day the great Cam Sorvino actually used the word *boyfriend* in reference to himself."

Cam threw a piece of sushi at her.

The conversation turned to milder topics as they whiled away the evening.

"By the way, how's your stocks and shares portfolio doing?" Cam asked Eveline sometime later.

Ethan stiffened slightly next to Joe. "I'll get us more drinks," he murmured. He rose from the table and headed for the bar.

"Oh, so-so," Eveline said with a casual air that had Joe narrowing his eyes.

He knew that expression. It was the one Eveline wore when she was hiding something.

"Mind if I take a look?" Cam said. "There's some pretty good stuff out there right now. You might be able to get on board before they go viral."

Eveline hesitated. She brought up an app on her cell and passed her phone to Cam.

Cam wiped his fingers clean and scrolled down the screen. His eyes widened.

"I see you've already got them."

"I do?" Eveline murmured with an innocent arch of her eyebrows.

Joe blinked.

Wow, whatever it is, it's a fucking whopper.

Cam stilled. He sat up and leaned an elbow on the table, gray eyes focusing as he flicked his finger down the screen.

"Seen enough?" Eveline said brightly. "Can I have my—"

"Wait up," Cam muttered, lines marring his brow as he studied the data on the cell. It was a full minute before he paused and leaned back in his chair. He watched Eveline with a hard expression. "Say, Eveline, you wouldn't happen to know a guy called Mr. S, would you?"

A loud clink came from the direction of the bar. Joe glanced to where Ethan stood behind the counter, his back to them while he mixed their drinks.

"Who's Mr. S?" Eveline asked, genuine puzzlement in her voice.

Cam frowned.

"He's one of our most elusive clients. Came out of left field about six years ago and wiped the floor with some of the best brains in the business in his first year of dealing in stocks and shares."

"Wow, Mr. S, huh?" Eveline muttered. "I'm afraid I don't know anyone by such a lame name."

There was a noise from the bar.

Joe looked to where Ethan was setting their glasses on a tray on the counter.

"You okay?"

"Uh-huh," Ethan murmured.

Surprise darted through Joe as he stared at Ethan.

Why are his ears so red?

"Really?" Cam said drily to Eveline. He pushed her

cell across the table. "'Cause the data on here pretty much mimics what he's been doing for the past few weeks."

Eveline grabbed her phone and slipped it inside her bag.

"Maybe my broker knows him."

Cam observed her for a silent moment.

"Maybe," he said finally. "Anyway, the guy would be seriously loaded if he didn't give most of his money away."

Eveline blinked.

"*What?*"

"Yup," Cam said with a dip of his chin. He took a sip of his Scotch. "He's a serious do-gooder. Donates most of it to this one charity that helps street kids around the world. Pretty neat for someone who nearly flunked Stanford business school."

Joe twitched. His eyes found Ethan where he was stiffly crossing the floor toward the table, tray in hand and downturned gaze focused on his feet.

"No, he didn't," Eveline blurted. "Ethan graduated summa cum laude. He got the fifth top score Stanford ever—*whoops!*" She clamped a hand over her mouth just as an almighty crash sounded.

Everyone startled bar Joe, who jumped to his feet and frowned at Ethan where he stood frozen in the middle of a sea of broken glass.

"You hurt?" Joe snapped.

Ethan shook his head, face pale and body immobilized under Joe's hard stare.

"Good," Joe said gruffly. "Don't move."

Joe's pulse started a steady drumming beat as he headed carefully across the shard-strewn floor to Ethan, his mind swinging between shock and anger at the outrageous revelation that had just slipped from Eveline's mouth.

"I'm sorry, Ethan," Eveline said with genuine regret. "I looked up your profile on—"

"No fucking way!" Cam exclaimed. *"You're telling me this little shit is Mr. S?!"*

"Hey, watch it!" Eveline growled. "This *'little shit'* made me a quarter million dollars last month."

"Wow," Gabe murmured.

Joe blocked out Cam's and Eveline's bickering as he reached Ethan.

Ethan licked his lips nervously.

"Um, Joe—"

The rest of Ethan's words vanished in a shocked whoosh when Joe grabbed his waist and tossed him over his shoulder. Joe held on to Ethan's butt and carefully navigated his way out of the danger area before turning toward the table where Cam, Gabe, and Eveline sat staring.

"Like a goddamn caveman," Eveline muttered in a voice full of admiration, her eyes dancing with laughter.

Cam grinned. Gabe soundlessly opened and closed his mouth beside him.

"Broom, dustpan, and mop are through there," Joe said silkily, indicating the private door next to the bar. He patted the firm ass of the man he was carrying. "This guy and I have some serious talking to do."

"Oh, fuck," Ethan whimpered.

Joe smiled grimly and headed for the back of the club, pleased with the small shiver that ran through his lover. He paused at a sudden thought, dug around in his pocket, and tossed something toward the table where their friends still sat.

"Oh, and lock up, will you?"

Cam caught the keys midair and chuckled. Gabe blushed beside him, his expression warming.

Joe caressed Ethan's ass, his fingers lingering lovingly on the tense toned flesh.

"We ain't coming down for the rest of the night. In fact, we might not leave the apartment for several days."

"Oh God!" Ethan groaned.

Eveline beamed. "Wow, your make-up sex is gonna be *so* hot."

Joe bit his lip to stop himself from laughing and moved toward the door. He nudged it open with his foot and carried on walking, not stopping until he reached the private stairs that led to his apartment. He ignored Ethan's mumbled protests while he climbed the steps, headed through the front door of his flat, and crossed the floor to his bedroom.

Joe tossed Ethan unceremoniously onto his freshly made bed before climbing up over him. He studied the flushed and clearly nervous man beneath him, wondering if he'd finally revealed the last of his secrets.

"So, you didn't flunk business school?" Joe said in a hard voice.

Ethan shook his head and licked his lips.

Joe's gaze dropped to Ethan's mouth, his cock stirring.

"And you're some kind of whiz kid?"

Ethan hesitated before shrugging and nodding, an awkward expression flashing across his face.

Joe stilled as he gazed into Ethan's eyes, the last of his irritation finally fading. Love filled him when he realized the gift Fate had granted him by bringing this sweet, funny, sexy, cocky, humble, brilliant man into his life.

Thank you, God!

Joe lowered his head and brought his lips to Ethan's left ear, prolonging his fake irate act just a bit longer.

"How much, Ethan?" he murmured.

Ethan shivered, his body reacting to Joe's touch. "What?" he mumbled in a dazed voice.

Joe licked the shell of Ethan's ear.

"How much are you worth?"

Ethan gasped and squirmed beneath him, his back arching.

"I—I don't want to—"

Joe tugged on the lobe of Ethan's ear with his teeth.

"Tell me."

Ethan moaned, hands rising to grip Joe's back. He whispered a figure that made Joe blink and freeze.

"Holy shit." Joe straightened and stared at Ethan. "And you've given most of it away?" he said hoarsely, his heart thumping wildly in his chest.

Ethan nodded.

"Why?" Joe blurted.

Ethan watched him for a long, silent moment, his eyes darkening as the seconds ticked by.

"Making money is a talent." Ethan touched Joe's face gently, his fingers skimming Joe's left cheek before coming to rest against his lips. "I'd rather be happy. With you."

Joe's breath hitched in his throat when he read the blatant adoration in Ethan's green eyes.

"God, you kill me."

Joe took Ethan's mouth in a scorching kiss that had the man beneath him clutching desperately at his shoulders.

"Any other secrets you need to tell me?"

Joe peeled his T-shirt off before tugging Ethan's out of his jeans and yanking it over his head.

Ethan feverishly undid Joe's belt buckle, his teeth sneaking out to tug sexily at his lower lip.

"What kind of secrets are we talking? Like stealing, cheating—"

Joe groaned when Ethan's fingers found his throbbing cock through his briefs.

"*Anything!*"

Ethan suddenly went quiet beneath him, a serious expression dawning on his face. He took a deep breath.

Joe tensed.

"I popped my cherry in the back of a Corolla," Ethan admitted solemnly.

Joe blinked before bursting out laughing. He couldn't believe how much fun sex with Ethan could be.

"I love you, Ethan Skye," he said after the last chuckle left his lips. "So goddamn much."

Ethan flushed, his gorgeous eyes filling with emotion at Joe's heartfelt confession. It was the first time Joe had openly declared his love to him. He raised trembling hands and cradled Joe's face.

"I love you, too, Joe Cavendish," he breathed.

Joe smiled and leaned down to kiss him.

THE END

What happens when Gabe Anderson dares to say the three little words that Cam Sorvino is scared to hear? Get the continuation to Gabe and Cam's story and find out today!

Get Tokyo Heat (Nights #3)
Turn the page to read an extract now!

TOKYO HEAT (NIGHTS SERIES BOOK 3) SPECIAL PREVIEW

CHAPTER ONE

SHIT!

Gabe gave his inbox a final glance, logged off, and rose from his desk. He glanced out of the panoramic windows to his left as he shrugged into his suit jacket.

Dusk cast red and orange streaks across the sky above Tokyo, the light washing through the glass and painting amber shadows on the crisp white walls of his office. He looked at his watch, cursed under his breath, and grabbed his bag.

He was five minutes late.

Gabe's gaze collided with a curious stare as he turned toward the door. A man with dark blond hair and blue eyes stood watching him, one shoulder propped against the frame.

"Got plans for the weekend?" he drawled, cocking an elegant eyebrow.

Gabe smiled, hoping his restlessness didn't show.

"Yes, I do."

Rhys Damon studied him for a moment longer before letting out a sigh.

"Ah, to be in love and shacked up."

Gabe felt his ears grow warm at his boss's teasing expression.

"I wouldn't go as far as that," he mumbled.

"I thought you'd moved in with him," Rhys said, surprise flashing in his blue gaze. "What's it been? Six months?"

"I did, and it's been six and a half," Gabe muttered.

Not that I'm counting.

He swallowed a groan at Rhys's sudden sly grin.

"I just sent you the final plans for the Hudson resort," Gabe said. "Let me know—"

"*Rhys!*" someone suddenly barked from across the expanse of the open-plan office space outside.

They turned and stared at the hulking, dark-haired man standing in the doorway of a glass room on the opposite side of the floor. Wade Tucker—the other brain behind the incredibly successful, multi-award-winning Chicago-based design firm currently taking Tokyo by storm—scowled at Rhys.

Rhys grimaced.

"It seems the big bad wolf has awakened." He glanced at Gabe. "Quick, run before he sinks his teeth into you too."

Gabe hurried toward the elevator and glanced over his shoulder at the two men facing each other stiffly across the empty office. He doubted he was the only one who had noticed the increasing tension between the firm's partners over the last year.

Best friends since their college days, Rhys Damon and Wade Tucker had followed in each other's footsteps throughout their early careers, often as rivals bidding for the same contracts. They'd finally set up shop as Damon & Tucker. Twelve years on and their company was now among the top twenty in the business for luxury interior design, consulting, and branding, catering to some of the most exclusive resorts and hotel chains around the world, as well as affluent private clients.

All thoughts of his bosses' woes fled Gabe's mind when he exited the lift and entered the lobby of the glass-and-steel edifice that housed the Tokyo branch of the firm.

A man stood leaning against a navy-blue Jaguar saloon parked at the curb outside, hands tucked in the pockets of his tailored suit and powerful legs crossed at the ankles. He seemed oblivious to the stares he was drawing from the passersby and office workers leaving the building, his eyes focused on the foyer.

Although the car was a stunning piece of art and engineering, Gabe knew it was its dark-haired owner who had captured the avid interest of the men and women openly ogling him.

Gabe's pulse jumped when he met the man's gunmetal stare through the glass wall. He still couldn't quite believe that he was going out with Cam Sorvino, the king of one-night stands. His gaze dropped from Cam's stunning face and full lips, to his stubbled jaw and hard physique.

Nor can I believe I've had sex with that gorgeous body.

Heat warmed Gabe's cheeks when he recalled the last time they'd shared a bed.

It had been over a week ago, a fact that had obviously frustrated Cam at the time as he barely let Gabe sleep that night. His job as an asset manager for one of the biggest investment firms in Asia had taken him to Singapore for most of the last month and he only returned to Tokyo on the weekends, often late on Saturday afternoons.

Though Gabe loved nothing more than being in Cam's arms, he knew the commute was taking its toll on his lover, which was why he'd asked Cam to fly back early this week.

Cam's gaze grew heavy-lidded as Gabe crossed the sidewalk and approached the car. Gabe knew that if it wasn't for the people around them, Cam would have pulled him into his embrace and kissed him senseless. Gabe stifled a sigh, somewhat grateful for their audience.

Once they started touching each other, there would be no stopping them. And Cam's libido had turned voracious as of late, his appetite not even remotely quenched until they'd had at least four rounds of toe-curling sex and Gabe's voice was hoarse from crying and moaning in pleasure.

"I've packed us a couple of overnight bags, like you instructed," Cam said in a smoky voice that sent tingles down Gabe's spine as he opened the passenger door of the Jag. "So, where are we headed, Mr. Anderson?"

Gabe slipped onto the cream leather seat and waited until Cam climbed in beside him before giving him the address of the place he'd booked them in for the weekend.

Cam raised an eyebrow.

"The beach?" His lips curved. "Does this mean I get to see you in swim trunks?"

Gabe's pulse skittered at the passionate gleam in the gray eyes watching him.

"It's a hot springs, so, no."

Cam grinned.

"Even better. You'll be naked."

Gabe rolled his eyes as Cam started the engine and steered the Jag around.

Although the drive to the Izu Peninsula took over two hours, the time flew by while they chatted about their week, soft jazz music playing from the speakers as the vehicle ate away the miles.

Cam's eyes widened when he drove into the paved courtyard of the traditional Japanese inn sitting on the small spur of land jutting out from the coastline, the headlights briefly illuminating the golden stretch of sand leading to the Pacific Ocean. He parked the car, his gaze lingering on the open vista before switching to Gabe.

"Nice."

Gabe smiled, a flutter of excitement sending his pulse racing at the night he'd planned for them.

"I'm glad you like it."

They collected their bags from the trunk and headed for the entrance.

Cam hesitated when they reached the porch, his hand on the handle of the front door.

"You didn't design this one too, did you?"

Gabe blinked. His ears grew hot as he suddenly recollected the exclusive Tokyo hotel where they'd first made love a year ago. It was where he'd also rather splendidly lost his cherry to the magnificent man beside him.

Gabe's cock twitched as he thought of that night. Though sex with Cam always blew his mind, their first time together was incredibly precious to Gabe.

It was Cam who had finally helped him overcome the trauma of his past, when he'd nearly been raped by five men who'd paid his then boyfriend to tape their vile acts on camera, leaving him unable to sleep with anyone for over eight years despite regularly seeing a therapist.

The gentle yet passionate way Cam had made love to him that time, how Cam had engraved his touch and scent on Gabe's body until he utterly and completely lost himself in the act, how he'd brought Gabe to one earth-shattering climax after another—all of it were priceless memories Gabe would take to his grave. Not that he would ever admit this to Cam.

Gabe chuckled at his lover's guarded expression.

"No, I didn't design this place."

Relief flashed across Cam's face.

"Good. I'd seriously feel as if I were committing blasphemy otherwise." Cam sniffed. "Not that sex with you isn't the most unholy, wicked thing I've ever experienced in my life. I mean, there's some stuff we've done that I—"

"Shut up, Cam!" Gabe hissed, clamping a hand over

Cam's mouth as a hostess headed across the foyer toward them.

Cam grinned and licked Gabe's palm. Gabe swallowed a groan at the tingle that shot through him.

This erotic asshole.

Read Tokyo Heat today

AFTERWORD

To all my friends who helped make this possible. You know who you are.

To you, my readers. Thank you for reading Ethan and Joe's story. I hope you loved this second book in the Nights series. I would be grateful if you could leave a review on Goodreads or on the store where you purchased this book. Reviews help readers like you find my books and I truly appreciate your honest opinions about my stories.

Make sure to sign up to my store newsletter for special deals on my books and new release alerts. Or you can sign up to my author newsletter instead to get upcoming release notifications, sneak peeks, and giveaways.

ABOUT THE AUTHOR

Ava Marie Salinger is the romance pen name of an Amazon bestselling author with a passion for writing addictive tales. Known for her action-packed and thrilling urban fantasy novels, she has expanded her repertoire with the introduction of the M/M urban fantasy romance series Fallen Messengers. Additionally, she has penned the scorching hot contemporary M/M romance series Nights and Twilight Falls as A.M. Salinger. When not immersed in her writing, Ava can be found curating inspiring music playlists, indulging in her love for nature, marveling at the latest gadgets, and savoring Chinese cuisine.

You can find all of Ava's books on her author store at shop.adstarrling.com